It is true to say that the glory of man is his capacity for damnation. The worst that can be said of most of our malefactors, from statesmen to thieves, is that they are not man enough to be damned.

—T. S. Eliot

I place my life on the same line with the enemy's. If damnation is the only prize, then let the Universe be the final judge. Meanwhile, I am the judgment.

—Mack Bolan, THE EXECUTIONER

The Executioner Series:

#1   WAR AGAINST THE MAFIA
#2   DEATH SQUAD
#3   BATTLE MASK
#4   MIAMI MASSACRE
#5   CONTINENTAL CONTRACT
#6   ASSAULT ON SOHO
#7   NIGHTMARE IN NEW YORK
#8   CHICAGO WIPEOUT
#9   VEGAS VENDETTA
#10 CARIBBEAN KILL
#11 CALIFORNIA HIT
#12 BOSTON BLITZ
#13 WASHINGTON I.O.U.
#14 SAN DIEGO SIEGE
#15 PANIC IN PHILLY
#16 SICILIAN SLAUGHTER
#17 JERSEY GUNS
#18 TEXAS STORM
#19 DETROIT DEATHWATCH
#20 NEW ORLEANS KNOCKOUT
#21 FIREBASE SEATTLE
#22 HAWAIIAN HELLGROUND
#23 ST. LOUIS SHOWDOWN
#24 CANADIAN CRISIS
#25 COLORADO KILL-ZONE
#26 ACAPULCO RAMPAGE
#27 DIXIE CONVOY
#28 SAVAGE FIRE
#29 COMMAND STRIKE
#30 CLEVELAND PIPELINE
#31 ARIZONA AMBUSH
#32 TENNESSEE SMASH
#33 MONDAY'S MOB
#34 TERRIBLE TUESDAY

THE

EXECUTIONER

TEXAS STORM

by
Don Pendleton

PINNACLE BOOKS • LOS ANGELES

THE EXECUTIONER: TEXAS STORM

Copyright © 1974 by Pinnacle Books, Inc.

An original Pinnacle Books edition, published for the first time anywhere.

ISBN: 0-523-40315-1

First printing, March 1974
Second printing, April 1978
Third printing, October 1978
Fourth printing, January 1979

Printed in the United States of America

PINNACLE BOOKS, INC.
2029 Century Park East
Los Angeles, California 90067

For Bolan's best friends of '73—
Cy and Frank, Scott and Jack.
Our thanks.

                                   —dp

TEXAS STORM

PROLOGUE

"I am not their judge. I am their judgment." With these words a Vietnam-baptized war machine who had already become known as the "Executioner" declared his personal war against the Mafia.

The motivation was as straightforward as the man himself. He had come to recognize that the universe provided its own balance: for every action there is a reaction, for every good an evil, for every strength a weakness—and for every injustice there was somewhere a final justice. By their own actions, the mob had provoked a reaction which was as inevitable and implacable as any force in the universe.

The mob itself had created this War Against the Mafia.

They had fashioned it from the stuff of which the Executioner was made and fanned it to life with the spreading flames of rampant thugdom.

The man was Mack Bolan. He was thirty years of age, a career soldier with two Southeast Asia tours behind him when he was called home to bury his parents and a teen-age sister, victims of Mafia terrorism. Bolan had grown up in the neighborhood where his family died. The Mafia was no stranger to him. He was acquainted with their omnipotence and viciousness. But he had been hardly more than a kid himself when he departed that environment. Consumed by the military problems of the larger world, Bolan had matured into manhood along the lines of military destiny, with little more than dim memories of that other world where violence and death also stalked the human footpaths.

The family tragedy abruptly jerked Executioner Bolan back into the reality of that dark landscape where thugdom reigned, focusing his attention upon the unrestrained plundering of that human estate ... and a new war was born.

> "I am not their judge.
> I am their *judgment!*"

It must have seemed to this formidable warrior that all the actions and interactions of his thirty years in life had been leading him inexorably along this collision course with that complex human cancer, the Mafia—known also as *La Cosa Nostra*, the syndicate, the combine, the mob. By whatever name, Bolan saw them collectively as a rapacious horde of thieves and cutthroats, plunderers, degraders of humanity, a destructive growth at the core of mankind. He also became strongly aware of the inability of the nation's legal structures to counteract this menace.

Someone, he knew, had to stand and fight.

Few men living at the time could have been more admirably equipped to assume the role that Bolan felt descending upon him.

10

He was, in his own understanding, particularly fit for the job. Something in his genetic makeup coupled with a peculiarly complex "toughness of the soul," and hardened by years of training and testing in a finite little hell called Southeast Asia had produced something truly unique in an individual human framework. Bolan knew himself. He knew what he could do. And he also knew what he *must* do.

This was not the first good man to run afoul of the cannibalistic activities of the organized crime world.

He was not the first to suffer personal tragedy, to see loved ones victimized, degraded, then sacrificed body and soul to the all-encompassing wave of this ever-advancing cancer.

Bolan was not even the first to stand and strike back.

But he was the first to be so magnificently equipped to handle the challenge. The challenge therefore became an obligation. It became, in every respect, a holy mission.

But Bolan was no philosopher. He would send you one of those humorously quizzical glances from his ice-blue eyes if you were even to suggest to his face that he was an idealist. Bolan would tell you that there is nothing so practical and real as survival. Jungle law is no philosophy—*it is reality;* this was Bolan's understanding. And the case at hand seemed entirely clear-cut in that understanding. The mob was out to rape the world and eat it whole. Nothing in the world was stopping them. Something or someone had to. Maybe Bolan could and maybe he could not. He was at least uniquely qualified to try. There was the commitment. Idealist, no. Realist . . . yeah, sure. All philosophical and moral questions to hell . . . *he had to try!*

And try he did.

He tried in seventeen consecutive pitched battles that ranged throughout the United States and spilled over into Europe, Britain, and the Caribbean. He engaged the enemy in a stunning and progressive application of one-man guerrilla warfare that left them reeling in confusion or stampeding in panic wherever he surfaced, and his formula for warfare became expressed in the simplest of expedients: Identify! Infiltrate or Isolate! Destroy!

His name quickly became a legend to the public, an inexhaustible source of interest to the news media, an embarrassing frustration to the law, a cussword filled with crawling fear to the mob.

Even so, all the world knew that Mack Bolan was a living dead man. His war was hopeless, his odds insurmountable, his chances for personal survival absolutely zero.

For every *Mafioso* who fell to his campaign, ten replacements stepped into the line. For each individual lawman who exhibited overt sympathy for the man and his war, a hundred became all the more determined to halt his illegal crusade. And for each small stolen moment of personal victory, Bolan himself realized that the odds against him thus pyramided in geometric progression.

But he kept trying.

And one day in late spring, when most of North America was awakening to the annual rebirth, a deadly storm came to the great state of Texas.

It was a human storm.

And its name was Bolan.

1: KNIGHT AT DAWN

The darkness of the Texas central plains was being diluted at its eastern edge by the mottled gray advance of dawn as a sleek, twin-engine Cessna swept across from the west, winging close above the flat landscape to maintain a low celestial profile.

Two men ocupied the aircraft.

The pilot was a dark, handsome young veteran of many low-profile flights such as this—both in the service of his country in adventures abroad, and in the service of others in adventures here at home. His name was Grimaldi. Until recently he had served the enemies of the man who now sat beside him.

The passenger wore black. He was garbed in a tight-fitting combat outfit of the type favored by those who must advance by stealth into hostile lands. At the moment he was a one-man raiding party. A military style web belt encircled his waist to support a heavy autoloading pistol plus various other weapons of war. Smaller belts angled from shoulders to waist in a crossing arrangement to accommodate miscellaneous munitions and accessories of survival. His face and hands were smeared with a black cosmetic. In the glow from the plane's instrument panel, only the eyes were clearly visible—steely glints of blue ice that seemed to see everything.

The pilot glanced at his passenger and suppressed an involuntary shiver. "Coming around on the midland omni," he announced solemnly.

The man in Executioner black did not immediately respond to the announcement, but a moment later calmly replied, "Bingo. Tank farm dead ahead."

Grimaldi said, "Right. Okay, get set. We're making a straight-in to the airstrip. You can mark it one minute and forty from the tank farm to touchdown."

The other man fiddled with a watch at his left wrist as he crisply delivered a repetitious instruction. "Keep it on the numbers, Jack. Give me ninety, exactly. Nine-oh."

"Sure, I know. That's from touchdown to full stop."

"That's what it is," the cold one growled, showing the first traces of emotion. "Unless you enjoy finding yourself in a cross fire."

"Nine-oh it is," Grimaldi replied with a tight smile.

The Executioner punched a timing stem on his watch as they flashed above a sprawling collection of oil storage tanks, then he began his last-minute countdown preparations. An enormous ammo clip clicked into position in the light chattergun that hung from his neck. Blackened fingers traced out once more the feel and position of munitions spaced along the utility belt while the other hand checked out the security of a waist weapon, the thunderous .44 AutoMag which—for this mission—was carrying scatter loads of fine buckshot. As a final item, a delicately engineered sound suppressor threaded its way onto the shoulder-slung "silent piece"—a 9-millimeter Beretta Brigadier which, through many campaigns, had become virtually an organ of the man and which he affectionately called "the Belle."

"That'd better be a *dirt* strip down there," he said, as though speaking for his own benefit.

Grimaldi chuckled nervously as he replied, "It was last time. But that's still mighty hard territory down there, man."

"It all is," the raider said. He sighed, very softly, and the blue ice glinted with some indefinable emotion. "Just get me in, and make all the dust you can. We'll take the rest one number at a time."

Sure. One number at a time. Grimaldi had seen plenty of Mack Bolan's "numbers"—in spades. Any way they fell out, it was nothing but bad news for the guys whose misfortune found them on the receiving end.

But what the hell? This was one of the best-guarded sites the guy could have chosen to hit. Why was it always the meanest ones?

Grimaldi had been there when the guy hit Vegas. And Grimaldi had been on the wrong side there.

He'd been there, also, during the Caribbean campaign—which actually had started out as no more than an extension of the Vegas thing. And, yeah, the dumb Italian had started out on the wrong side in Puerto Rico, too.

So what about *this* time? Grimaldi shrugged away a little quiver of apprehension and aligned the nose of the aircraft with the tiny dirt strip that came into

16

view just ahead. His hands and mind were going to be very busy for the next minute or so, and for that he was thankful. As for the rest of it . . . right or wrong, Mack Bolan was his man. There simply was no other way to think of it.

"Gear down," he announced quietly.

Bolan released his seat belt and reminded the pilot, "Start your count when I go out the door."

"Sure," Grimaldi replied.

Oh, sure. They might have been discussing when to meet for dinner, it was that casual. But that hell-fire guy was going to go out that door with blood on his mind. He was dropping into a Mafia hardsite with no less than a dozen pro killers defending it and with God only knew how many local recruits to back them up—and he was going to be hitting that earth out there with every intention of scorching it or dying in the attempt.

And for what?

For what damned possible good?

It seemed to Grimaldi like a hell of a way to live . . . or die.

He brought the nose up and cut the power. Then the wheels touched and a cloud of dust swirled into the slipstream.

"There's your cover, Mr. Blitz," he intoned, the words sounding loud and overly dramatic in the sudden silence of the dead-stick landing.

A dimly lit shack flashed past on his left; his peripheral vision caught unmistakable movement—*human* movement—as floodlights erupted on all sides.

17

Then he was braking for the turnaround as the door cracked open at the far side of the cabin.

The man in black called, "Tallyho, Jack."

Tallyho, yeah. A hunting cry. The guy was gone in a flash of ice-blue eyes. The cabin door closed with a quiet click. And Jack Grimaldi had just brought a very hot war to the peaceful state of Texas.

Something was rotten in Texas.

Bolan did not know precisely what that something was.

He did know, though, that a strongly apparent odor was emerging from this particular spot on the Texas midlands, one of the nation's chief oil-producing areas, and that the odor was being experienced at some rather disconcerting points throughout this wealthy state.

Klingman's Wells had once been among the most productive oil leases in the midlands. Not now. Several months back, the rich wells of Klingman Petro had abruptly gone out of production, much to the surprise of other oilmen in the area. And an air of mystery had settled upon the place.

Rumors had it that the old man's daughter had disappeared and that Klingman himself had gone into virtual seclusion in his Dallas apartment. That in itself was mystery enough. Arthur Klingman was one of the pioneer Texas oilmen, one of the last great independents in this age of corporate giants, a tough old desert rat who could not stand the smell of plush offices and mahoganied board rooms.

Mack Bolan did not like mysteries, particularly

when they involved mob operations. And Klingman's Wells was now without a doubt a very important mob centerpoint. Whatever the nature of the new activities, quite obviously it was more profitable and therefore more desirable than the harvesting of fossil fuels.

The most painstaking investigation had failed to reveal to the Executioner's curious mind the true name of the Mafia game in Texas. But there was more than one way to gain intelligence; if you couldn't pry it loose then maybe you could blast it into the open. And that was the real nature of this daring dawn strike at a mob command post; it was shock therapy, to be delivered in Bolan's inimitable style of blockbuster warfare. The shock waves just might rattle something loose and into the intelligence network.

So—if Bolan had heard Jack Grimaldi's silent question, *For what damned possible good?*—he could have replied, "Not for good, Jack, but for bad. When you have an omnipotent enemy then you simply hit him with everything you can grab—you give him all the *bad* you can muster—and then you check for leaks in that shell of power."

Bolan was here for some damned possible bad.

He had been here many times—but only on paper. He knew this terrain as though he had lived here a lifetime, and he was intimate with each structure, fixture, and device within that compound—thanks mainly to the remarkable memory of Jack Grimaldi, who had chauffeured several flights of Mafia bosses to the site just after the takeover.

At the moment, Grimaldi was providing some distracting maneuvers with the taxiing aircraft. Bolan was on the lee side of the dust screen and galloping along the backtrack—the chattergun riding in muzzle-down standby, the silent Beretta Belle in hand and at the ready, and he was closing vital numbers on the growing collection of sounds up there in that confused jumble of sand-polluted darkness and choked floodlights.

The timing could not have been more precise. It was the moment that divided night from day, with just the faintest sliver of gray light moving into the eastern heavens. Bolan had learned long ago that this was the best possible time to catch an enemy off its guard, especially those who have watched through the long and uncertain night.

And now the sounds up there in that tail of the night were beginning to assimilate themselves for the alert ears that had come in with the dawn.

A guttural voice that bore no trace of Texas twang was loudly demanding to know the identity of the landing plane.

Another voice, calling from somewhere on Bolan's side of the runway, replied that the craft was ". . . that Cessna, I think. You know—the Three-Ten, the twin-engine job."

"Must be Detroit," the first voice decided, showing a tint of nervousness. "Wonder who it is this time. Somebody get that radio—you mean to say he didn't even identify hisself?"

Bolan had not slowed his pace, and now he was almost directly across from the point of reception,

20

moving into the floodlit area. The outline of a low-slung building was framed out over there in the thin slice of gray horizon, a floodlight atop the building sending a swirling beam through dust-laden atmosphere. Without breaking stride he squeezed off two sighing messengers of darkness from the Beretta. The quiet coughing of the Belle mingled with and was absorbed by the explosive shattering of the floodlight.

In that moment of flare-out a startled face loomed into Bolan's restricted field of vision, a visage obviously more at home on a Manhattan waterfront than at this unlikely outpost of civilization.

The guy had spotted Bolan first—may have even heard the gasping reports of the Beretta. His mouth was open in a silent cry and he was flinging himself into a grotesque pirouette while trying to bring a long-barreled revolver to bear on this unsettling apparition from the night. But then the light was gone, Bolan had closed that short range, and the soldier from Manhattan became a shattering reed in the grip of an implacable force which bent him double, cracked his spine, and snuffed out the candle of life as quietly and as quickly as two fingers closing on a wick.

The only sound from the lightning encounter was a despairing *whu-uff* as a life took flight and the oddly twisted body sagged to earth.

Across the runway, someone was declaring, "Hell, the damn light blew out."

Several other edgy voices were commenting on the fact, revealing presences which until that time Bolan

21

could but guess at—five or six men, spaced at irregular intervals in a more or less straight line along the other side of the landing strip.

But there were closer ones. Another form materialized immediately from the graying darkness on Bolan's side. The guy cried, "Hey! What is—?"

A 9-millimeter zinger spat across the grayness and between parted teeth to explode in a red fountain of displaced matter, the interrupted question finding a ready answer in the gentle *phu-uut* of the sighing Beretta.

This one died loudly, with a bubbling scream accompanying the backward pitch and rattling return to sources.

The gravel voice from across the way yelled, "What the hell is going on over there?"

So okay. Not just the way he would prefer it, but okay.

This was as far as silent lightning would take him on this mission.

Bolan returned the Beretta to sideleather.

It was time for thunder.

Not counting a few extra inches provided by the Western boots which he had adopted immediately upon his arrival in Texas, Jim "Woofer" Tolucci stood an even five and one-half feet tall. He weighed two hundred and forty very solid pounds—and the face atop that burly frame, even in repose, bespoke a man of seething energies and thinly veiled ferocity.

Tolucci was "head cock" at Klingman's Wells. The garrison force of Mexican nationals had addressed him as *Capitain* since his arrival at the hardsite. It was a tag which obviously pleased this graduate of big city street wars. The hardmen of his personal Mafia cadre sometimes used the term in an ingratiating sense, though not always to good effect. In private moments, the *Mafiosi* referred to their boss as "the animal." In kinder moments he was "Woofer"—but always, in direct address, "Mr. Tolucci."

The Woofer had already committed every crime in the book, including several murders, when he was "made" by the mob at the age of twenty. He was not considered overly bright, not even by the lieutenant who sponsored his initiation, but there was no denying the animal cunning and instinctive ferocity that assured Jim Tolucci a valued place in the organization.

He inherited his nickname at the age of twenty-five as a result of an injury suffered during a beer hall free-for-all. Someone had worked over his throat with the jagged edges of a broken bottle, causing irreparable damage to his vocal chords. The effect on his speech was a gravelly basso which could be neither modulated nor softened; his every word was a bark. During exertion or unusual emotional stress, each movement of his respiratory system produced a clearly audible and deep-throated growling.

At this moment *El Capitain's* growling was continuous, and his barking commands could be heard throughout the compound.

"Never mind the light now! It's almost daylight!"

And, an instant later: "Mickey! Take some *vaqueros* down there and check out that plane! What'sa

23

matter with that guy? Something's damn funny here! Hasn't that guy called in yet? Get on that fuckin' radio and—!"

This last instruction was interrupted by a gurgling scream emanating from somewhere out in the darkness, across the runway toward the west fence.

Tolucci took a lunging step in that direction then froze to throw back his head and bawl, "What the hell is going on over there!"

Receiving no immediate response, he dispatched three of his boys to that quarter with the wave of an arm and the rasping command: "Check it out!"

But then something very weird happened.

The aircraft hangar and office, just a few paces to Tolucci's rear, went up in a flaming explosion.

The concussion of the blast sent the head cock sprawling to hands and knees. Before numbed reflexes could even begin to assess the situation, a secondary explosion—caused probably by the touching-off of the hangar's aviation fuel storage—rattled the air and sent fiery droplets raining everywhere.

But Tolucci had no time to ponder that event, either. A piece of the disintegrating building descended upon the kneeling figure, flattening it in the dust of Texas—and just as all the lights were going out, *El Capitain* could have sworn that he caught a glimpse of a tall figure in black, illuminated by the flames of the blazing building, striding coolly into the holocaust with a chopper under his arm and spitting hellfire at everything.

But shit!

That couldn't be possible.

It just wasn't possible.

Bolan himself at that moment was not wondering just how possible it all was. The hastily flung grenade had evidently found a vital spot; the secondary gasoline explosion had come in right on the numbers—and the mission, at this point, was an unqualified *go*.

He went—with the chattergun blazing the trail through her flame-wreathed muzzle with coolly timed bursts that were seeking and finding maximum effect.

People were staggering and reeling around over there, totally disorganized and seized by the trauma of *blitzkrieg* assault.

Yeah.

It was entirely possible.

She awoke with a start and lay very still for a few seconds while attempting to recapture the whatever that had awakened her; then quickly she switched on the small bedside lamp.

It came again, then, a *whoofing* explosion that brightened the skies outside and sent shadows dancing across the walls of her room.

Gunfire, now, and the unmistakable staccato of a machine gun. Men yelling and screaming.

It sounded like—down at the hangar.

Footsteps running past her door. Voices raised in hysterical Spanish. Shadowy figures floating past the window, pounding feet, frenzied commands well sprinkled with obscenities.

More gunfire, closer now—the sudden big booming of some unimaginable weapon.

Thank God. Oh, thank God.

She slid to her feet, draped the thin blanket across her shoulders to cover her nakedness, and willed her legs to be steady as she staggered to the door.

Her mind seemed clear enough; it was just the body that would not act properly.

The door was still locked. Damn it, it was still locked.

She pounded on it ineffectually for a moment, then returned to the bed, carefully moved the lamp to the floor, and hurled the small table at the window with all the strength she could gather.

The window shattered. The table rebounded from the steel mesh outside and knocked her sprawling.

Another huge boom sounded from just outside the broken window. Someone screamed and footfalls again passed her door, this time moving quickly toward the rear.

The girl pulled herself to her feet and was trying to get herself properly wrapped inside the blanket when she became aware of someone standing just outside the shattered window, peering in at her.

A black face, with blazing eyes.

She shuddered and tried to say something to the face, but her voice would not work.

Then abruptly there was nothing at that window, nothing at all, and she wondered if there ever had been.

Another loud explosion rocked the building. An acrid stench drifted in through the window.

More yelling, pounding feet, a fast volley of gun-fire—sudden silence.

She stood in the center of the room, swaying in the blanket, eyes focused on that door, and prayed for a miracle.

And then the door opened with a crash and a tall commando stood there—a big silver pistol filling one of his hands—other guns and stuff hanging all over him—the face blackened—and, yes, she had actually seen the thing at the window.

Imagine that. She'd prayed for a miracle and received a commando. Was she dreaming some old British war movie?

The apparition was speaking to her, but it didn't sound very British. "Are you Miss Klingman?"

The blanket was slipping off the shoulders and gaping in embarrassing places.

She said, "Yes," but the voice didn't sound much like Judith Klingman's. She was struggling with the blanket and trying very hard to behave intelligently. "I'm not—not—they took my clothes and gave me drugs. Wh-who're you?"

"My name is Bolan," he told her. "I guess I've come for you."

Imagine that. A black knight had come for her.

No armor, just shining eyes.

She said, "Thank you," lost the battle for the blanket, and fainted dead away.

2: THE TALLY

The withdrawal from Klingman's Wells was a real hair-raiser. Grimaldi had pulled the plane to within a hundred feet of the flaming debris that littered the runway and wheeled about in preparation for the quick, short takeoff roll.

Bolan had obviously overplayed his numbers and the opposition was beginning to reorganize itself. He had to shoot a couple of dungareed dudes off the boarding ladder before he could hoist the unconscious girl into the pilot's waiting arms—then Grimaldi sent the hot little craft careening down the strip to the accompaniment of crackling following fire while Bolan knelt with the girl between the seats.

They became airborne just in time to clear the fence—by inches. The next hazard was a drilling tower, directly in the line of flight—again, a miss by the seat of Grimaldi's pants—but then they were up and clear and circling eastward.

The pilot passed trembling fingers across his eyes and muttered, "Damn! You do call 'em close." His gaze drifted magnetically to the nude beauty who Bolan at that moment was rebundling into the blanket. "But interesting, yeah," he added, with a strained chuckle.

Bolan strapped the unconscious bundle into a rear seat, then dropped his own frame into the copilot position and let out a long, tired sigh as he unburdened himself of armaments.

Grimaldi waited as long as he could, biting his lip and busying himself with the radionavigational equipment. He lined into the course to the Webb AFB vortac then lit a cigarette and blew the smoke sideways toward his friend. "Well, damn it, are you going to tell me about it?"

"Scrubbed out at Target Central," the man in black replied, the voice utterly devoid of emotion. "Civilians on board. Women, old men. Even heard a kid crying."

'Sorry 'bout that," Grimaldi said, using the same flat tone of voice. "Weren't there my last time in."

"Garrison people," Bolan told him. "I should have guessed. The Mexicans. They like their womenfolk close by."

The pilot took a long pull on the cigarette and darted a glance toward the rear of the plane. "So how do you rate the hit?" he asked nervously.

Bolan slowly shook his head, obviously pondering the same question. "Too soon to say, I guess." He lit a cigarette for himself and took several quick drags before adding, "Aren't you going to ask about the booty?"

"I figured you'd get to that," the pilot replied soberly.

"I think she's Judith Klingman."

"The hell!"

"Yeah. Locked in a bedroom at the *hacienda*."

Grimaldi made a sound through pursed lips and

tossed another quick glance over his shoulder. "In that condition?"

Bolan's head jerked in a quick nod. "Just about. She was on her feet when I busted in, but just. Said something about drugs. She was a prisoner, no mistake."

Grimaldi's eyes were studying the instrument panel, but obviously his mind was focused elsewhere. Presently, he asked, "Did you get the animal?"

"I don't know," Bolan truthfully answered. "I heard him, during the quiet drill. Then things got hot and suddenly I wasn't hearing him anymore. I don't know, Jack."

"I'd feel better with that one verified," the Mafia pilot declared. "He'd never qualify as the smartest gun in the West, but that guy has a sixth sense about some things."

Bolan said, "Yeah."

"Judith Klingman, eh?"

"I think so. And I think she verified it."

"Well . . ." Grimaldi was thinking about that, eyes crackling as the mind massaged the situation. He said, "I guess that could explain a few things."

"Yeah," Bolan agreed.

"I read it as a hell of a good break."

"So do I," Bolan said. "Also a hell of a problem."

"Uh . . . yeah. I see what you mean. Okay. So what's next?"

Bolan stared at the glowing tip of his cigarette for a moment, then replied, "First off, Jack, I want you to safe it. I left a lot of survivors back there. Sorry, but that's the way the ball bounced. Somebody could have a good make on this plane. You'll have to cover that."

"Okay," Grimaldi quickly agreed. "I'll bury it. I know a guy up in New Mexico. He'll log it in for me, any date I say. I'll have him tear down the engines and log 'er in for maintenance, as of yesterday."

"Great."

"Sure, it'll work. Then I'll pick up some more wings and hot it on over to Dallas. Wait for your call there. Okay?"

Bolan was thinking about it. He crushed out the cigarette and allowed a bit of emotion into the voice as he regretfully replied, "Maybe you better just bail on out of this one."

"No need for that," Grimaldi came right back. "I can cover it. Look, I'm available. Use me."

"I can't cover you, Jack. And if the boys get even a sniff—well, you know."

The pilot grimaced at the thought. "Yeah, I know."

Sure, Grimaldi knew.

The "boys" would enjoy nothing better than a free whack at Mack Bolan's head. Bolan knew and Grimaldi knew—the mob would skin alive one of their own brothers and feed him his own fingers if they even suspected that he had information which would lead them to their most hated enemy.

Grimaldi was not even a "made" man. He was simply an employee, a hired chauffeur with wings. Yeah. They'd roast him on an open spit and thoroughly enjoy every screaming moment of it . . . and there would be many long screaming moments.

Grimaldi shuddered. "Maybe you'd better scrub

31

out the whole trip," he muttered. "I'm getting a bad feeling about this state. It's too open, too damned big—and I get the feeling there's too much at stake here, for the boys. Every boss in the country has been down here within the past few months. They must be smelling money, and I mean big money."

"All the more reason for me," Bolan said. "You know I can't walk away."

"Well I can't bail out on you, man!"

Bolan grinned wryly. "Sure you can."

"So what if I do? What about you? Playing it by ear from here?"

"It's about all I've got," Bolan told him.

"What about the girl?"

"She's the starter, I guess. First, though, I want to get her to a medic. Know one?"

"You mean a quiet one. Not within a thousand miles, no."

"Then I'll have to scratch one up."

"Think she may be overdosed?"

"There's that possibility. I can't overlook it. First I check her out. Then I'll check her into the problem."

"Maybe she knows nothing. I mean nothing."

"I'm betting she does," Bolan said.

"You may be betting your life."

"So what's new?"

Grimaldi laughed sourly. He squinted at the instrument panel and announced, "Big Spring coming up. You'd better get ready."

The next few minutes were silent ones. Bolan was

32

stowing weapons and pulling street clothes on over the skin suit.

The girl moaned once and said something in gibberish.

Grimaldi was studying the terrain below, looking for visual orientation toward their destination, a small private airfield just north of Big Spring.

A military jet passed to starboard and waggled wings at them. Grimaldi waggled back and told his passenger, "Okay. Military control zone just ahead. I'm starting around. Make it three minutes to touch-down."

"Make it four minutes and fly by once, Jack," Bolan said quietly. "I want a look, at five hundred feet."

Grimaldi grinned, his good humor returning in a rush. What the hell, this was *Mack Bolan* sitting here. This guy didn't *bet* anything. He *invested,* very carefully.

The fiery glow of the Texas sun was making its debut on the terrestrial horizon, unmindful of the storm clouds gathering across that landscape. Tally-ho, hell yes. A hunted landscape.

A scrub-out at Klingman's Wells?

The tough little Italian who'd been everywhere and seen it all shivered and set his mental perspectives in order.

Somebody should ask the survivors back there about that so-called scrub-out.

Grimaldi smiled into the sun and said, "Looks like a nice day, Sarge."

"Every day is," Bolan replied.

Yeah. Grimaldi understood that, too. For a guy who lived from one heartbeat to the next, every day just had to be something special. Today is the rest of your life, eh? Okay. So okay.

"I'll be in Dallas," he told the large-lifer beside him; then he began the descent for the 500-foot recon into that next heartbeat.

3: COUNTER MOVE

Joseph Quaso had been Chief Enforcer of the Texas Territory for only about six months, but already he had built quite a reputation for himself in the organization. He was young, tough, energetic, and—most importantly—he knew how to use his head.

Quaso was a new-breed *Mafioso*, one of the young swinging Turks who were fast moving into positions of importance in most of the old Mafia families. His ties were with the Detroit coalition, and they were blood ties. He was kid-brother to Anthony Quaso, an "administrator" under Crazy Sal Vincenti, who was one of the lesser lights in the Detroit ruling council.

The Texas job was a *Commissione* appointment. Texas was regarded as an "open territory"—which simply meant that all of the families had the right to stake claims there. The Detroit council had strongly sponsored their fair-haired up-and-comer for the appointment and the other bosses of the national commission had accepted him without reservation.

And it was a big job. In every practical respect, young Joseph Quaso (age twenty-eight) was the boss of Texas. He was "man on the scene" for *La Commissione*. As such, it was his primary responsibility to orchestrate the Texas interests of the various families—to do so in a fair and impartial manner—

to keep the peace and promote harmony between competitive interests—and to protect the overall combination from unfavorable outside influences.

It was a Gestapo job.

And "Jaunty Joe" Quaso loved every nuance of it.

He commanded a standing army which had recently swelled to an estimated force of more than one hundred guns; he had unlimited financial resources for his "national security budget"; and—best of all—he had the undivided respect and support of the old men throughout the country.

This Texas phenomenon ruled his empire from an $1,100 per month penthouse in a Dallas suburb, a sprawling eight-room palace. Special feature of the sumptuous apartment was the monstrous bedroom of the master suite. It boasted a revolving playboy bed with built-in bar and quadrophonic sound system, television, and a special toy consisting of a closed-circuit TV camera and monitor with video-taping capabilities. Also available, at the flick of a switch on the master control panel, was a cartridge-style movie projector with an infinite variety of porno films—many of them "produced" by Quaso himself during an earlier period of "self-discovery."

The Boss Enforcer was, by tradition, forbidden to operate business sidelines of his own which might represent a conflict of interest. This did not, however, prevent Jaunty Joe from establishing a "Super-chick Corps" to service the Dallas-Fort Worth area of big spenders. In the official book, "Superchick" was a "grease operation"—that is, for the entertainment of important officials in local governments and key industries—a bribery device. It was common knowledge, though, that the Superchicks were also providing a handsome sideline income for the Gestapo chief of Texas. The national bosses were aware of this, and it is a testament to Quaso's popularity within the national council that none felt moved to slap the youngster down for the impropriety.

Besides, the Superchicks had been a brilliant addition to the clout operations in the new territory. Money was, of course, king when it came to winning official friends and influencing important people. But not every man could be reached with money alone. Few, however, could resist the added allure of a full-boobed and high-assed Texas beauty, available upon request for a couple of spins upon the revolving bed. And then, even if the pigeon didn't feel particularly grateful for the experience, there was always the very interesting cartridge film which inevitably recorded the event and which never failed to bring around the ungrateful ones.

Quaso himself was not exactly immune to the charms of the Superchicks. It is said that one or two, sometimes three or four, were usually "in residence" at the Quaso pad. On a revolving basis, of course. Jaunty Joe could not stomach the same woman two nights in a row. There were times, it is also said, when nothing less than several at once could sufficiently "relax" the libidinous young Turk from Detroit and ensure him a decent night's sleep.

It was the added misfortune of Jim "The Animal" Tolucci that his early morning call from Klingman's

Wells came on the heels of a fitful and misspent night in that Dallas penthouse.

Another of the problems lay in Tolucci's own agitated state of mind.

"What the hell are you telling me, Woofer?" Quaso said irritably into the telephone. He glanced at the clock in the control panel and groaned, then kicked the tousled bedcovers away and swung his feet to the floor. "Say that again, and calm down while you do it. I can't hear a damn thing through all that growling. Do you know what time it is?"

"Yessir, I know what time it is," the Woofer barked back. "Calm down hell, sir. All hell has broke down here. Listen, I'm lucky I'm alive. That guy romped in here and—"

"Wait, hold it. Start again. *What* guy?"

"I told you, that Bolan bastard! He was here. He blew up the goddam hangar and shot the shit out of everything! I'm lucky I'm alive!"

"I guess you are," Quaso said tensely. He took time to light a cigarette, then interrupted another unintelligible rush of barks and growls to say, "Okay, shut up and listen to me. Cool it, now. I can't understand a thing you're saying. Is the guy dead or alive?"

"What? What guy?"

"Bolan, you dummy! What the hell—didn't you say—?"

"Yessir. It was him, all right. A dozen people saw him. I saw 'im myself, it was him. He come in here just about—"

"Wait, damn it, Woofer, shut up!" Quaso was

beginning to understand the message now, but he really did not wish to. "Are you saying the guy hit you and got away? Out there in the middle of fucking nowhere? He got away?"

"Yessir. He flew, see. The bastard flew in and flew out. He flew. I didn't see the damn—"

"Woofer, shut up! Now shut up! Start all over again!"

". . . that Three-Ten out of Detroit, we think. And he took the broad."

"You squawking greaseball, *shut up!* I can't understand a—what? He took what?"

"Yessir, he took the broad. I guess. We searched everywhere. We can't find—"

"Woofer, he snatched the Klingman chick?"

"Yessir, that's all we can figure. But listen! We need to get after that plane. It was that Cessna out of—"

"Woofer goddamn it shut up and just answer me when I tell you to. Now listen to me. You keep this quiet. Not a word, not a goddamned word, you hear me? You tell nobody. I'm sending you some reinforcements and I—"

"Christ, sir, we don't need 'em now. We need to—"

"I said shut up! I'm taking it over. You just sit tight, I'm sending a crew over."

Quaso banged the receiver into its cradle then punched the call button for his house man and leapt to his feet. He was halfway to the bathroom when the bodyguard appeared in the other doorway.

"Yeah, boss?" the tagman reported, his eyes averted from the display of bossly nudity.

"Get ahold of that guy in Austin," Quaso commanded. "Tell him to hold the phone, I'll be right there. Try the home number first, he's probably still in bed—oh, and also that guy on the airport commission. And get ahold of Larry Awful. Tell him it's an alert, full scale, statewide. I want all his guns on the line. And call the Klingman drop. Tell them no privileges, especially no phone calls and no visitors until they hear from me again. Then roust the Superchicks and run them out of here. Oh, and you better get ahold of our man at city hall. Tell him I want him here in thirty minutes, no fail. Then— no, never mind, I'll do the rest."

The houseman nodded his understanding of the instructions and went to the telephone.

Quaso continued on to the bathroom. He stared darkly at his bladder-relieving waterfall and said, softly, to himself, "Okay, okay."

The honeymoon in Texas was over.

It was time to start earning his keep.

And, sure, it was going to be a pleasure. Better, even, than Superchicks.

4: ONE MORE TIME

Paul Hensley had just completed an unusually early morning round of his patients at Community Memorial Hospital. He signed out at the doctors' desk, picked up his medical bag, and went out through the emergency entrance to the parking lot.

He squinted briefly into the rising sun, thought briefly of the elderly lady in the cardiac ward who would probably die without seeing another sunrise, then sighed and went on toward his car.

There were times when Hensley very decidedly disliked being a doctor. He had lost two patients during the night—and he was about to lose a third. All those grieved relatives—standing grimly by throughout the deathwatch—looking at him every time he entered the room with *that* look, that *why-the-hell-can't-you-do-something* look.

Anyone with a God complex should take up doctoring.

It was one of the first things a physician must learn. He was not God.

Splint, patch, bandage, cut, sew, swab—look, grunt, uh-uhm, prescribe—and after that, what?

After that you stood helplessly by and watched them die, if die they must.

Yes, there were times when Doctor Paul would rather be a plumber.

41

He had one hand on the door of the car and was fishing for keys with the other hand when a tall young man appeared from nowhere and lightly touched his shoulder. Later, Hensley would remember the neat, tailored look of the sky-blue suit, the casual grace with which the man moved, the quiet force of his speech. At the moment, the doctor was simply in a lost-patient funk and in no frame of mind to consciously note such things. Also he was a bit irritated over the fact that the man was wearing smoked glasses, an obvious affectation at this time of day.

"Are you a doctor?" the tall one asked him.

Hensley's eyes flicked to the medical bag which he had deposited on the roof of the car. For one bitterly silly moment he wanted to reply that no, he was not a doctor, he was a medical bag's caddy. But he turned full around and stared at his own reflection in the smoked lens and told the sunglass kid, "Yes. Do you need attention?"

"I don't," the man replied. "But a friend does. In a vehicle over here. Will you come with me?"

The irritation became greater. Come wave a wand over someone's head, eh? Pull something from the medical bag of tricks and perform a Godly chore? "That's the emergency entrance right behind you," he said aloud. "Take your friend in there. They'll take care of him."

The man removed the sunglasses. Hensley was startled by the force of those eyes as the man asked him, "Does this face mean anything to you, Doctor?"

Should it? Vaguely, something there which . . . in

the newspapers?—a magazine cover, maybe? Hensley shook his head. "The emergency—"

"My name is Bolan. Does that mean anything?"

"You should take your friend—did you say Bolan?"

Of course, of course. Suddenly nervous and flustered, now, the doctor reached for a cigarette, then hastily changed his mind and let the hand fall to his side in clear view.

"I guess it does," the tall one said. He replaced the sunglasses and handed another pair to Hensley. These had lenses of opaque black, curved in at the temples to completely shut out all light. "Put the glasses on, Doctor. Simple security. I won't put a gun to your head. But my friend does need a medic. Will you come with me?"

Without a word, Hensley donned the opaque lenses and held out an arm. The man took it and led him away.

The doctor for some reason or other counted the paces. There were twenty-three. There was no conversation during the march. Except for the pressure of the hand on his arm, there was nothing even to mark the presence of the other man—no sound of footsteps other than his own, no rustling, no breathing, nothing.

Then came the metallic sound of a door being opened. His guide instructed him to "step high, and watch the overhead."

And then Mack Bolan—the most hotly sought man in the country—removed the glasses from the doctor's eyes and handed him the medical bag.

They were inside a small van-type truck. The

light in the van section was bad, but not so bad that Hensley could not see the blanket-draped figure on a fold-down bunk. It was a young woman with long blonde hair. She was unconscious. Above her, secured to the wall with metal clips, was a fantastic arsenal of weapons—all arranged in neat and handy rows. Something that looked suspiciously like the business end of a bazooka protruded from beneath the bunk on which the woman lay. All along the opposite wall were a miscellany of war munitions. Ammunition boxes and other stuff was neatly stacked on the floor, leaving very little standing room.

Hensley opened his bag and crouched beside the bunk. "There's not enough light in here," he complained.

Bolan flicked on a battery-operated lantern. "Best I can offer," he said. "I've seen battlefield surgeons take a man apart and reassemble him in worse light than this."

"Yes," Hensley murmured. "So have I." He opened the blanket and took the girl's pulse, then he peeled back an eyelid and tested for pupillary reflex.

"She's mildly comatose," the doctor reported, flicking a glance at his interested host.

"How mildly?"

"She should be hospitalized."

"What would you do for her in there?"

"Observation, medication. The usual things." Uh-huh, and wait for God to make the disposition. Bolan was giving him that cold stare. He added, "We'd have to make tests. Then the treatment would depend upon what the tests revealed."

"Which battlefield do you remember, Doctor? Vietnam?"

"No. Korea. I was a corpsman, Fleet Marine Force. Decided there was something better than dragging a stretcher across war-torn lands. Tried medical school, GI Bill. So here I am, having discovered that it's *all* war-torn land. What brings you to our state, Mr. Bolan?"

"Maybe she did," the tall man replied, that penetrating gaze shifting to the girl. "Your cure could be her killing, Doctor—if it means you have to hospitalize her. I just pulled this girl out of some kind of hell. The people I took her from won't be taking kindly to that. They'll be trying to get her back. So we need a battlefield decision here."

"Just how good a friend is she?" the doctor wondered aloud.

"We've never met," the big guy replied. "I found her in this condition. But I'm not leaving her this way."

"I'm going to light a cigarette," the doctor announced quietly.

"Go ahead."

"I was just wondering if it was safe. I mean, on top of all this gunpowder."

"It's safe," the cold one assured him.

Hensley lit the cigarette, glanced at the surgeon general's warning on the pack, and muttered, "Everyone dies of something." Then he told Bolan, "I don't know what you're doing in Texas, mister, but I can tell you that you're better off somewhere else—anywhere else. The FBI and the local police have papered this whole area with artists' sketches of your face—and it's a pretty good likeness. They even sent one to my office—and I'm sure I saw one down at the admissions desk of this hospital."

"Like you said," Bolan replied, "it's *all* war-torn land."

The doctor shrugged and said, "True, true. Well . . ."

"Let's say that we're in Korea," Bolan said, "ten miles from the field hospital. We're pinned down by enemy fire. What do we do for our patient?"

The doctor sighed. He used his pencil-flash to examine the girl's arms, then he sighed again. "Is she an addict?" he asked.

"I don't believe she gave herself those needle marks. She was a prisoner, under lock and key."

"Have you any idea at all what drug was being used?"

Bolan shook his head. "No. But the idea, I guess, was to keep her quiet."

Hensley removed a syringe from the medical bag and told the other man, "You're going to have to trust me, Mr. Bolan. For just about ten minutes. I want a blood analysis. I can't prescribe without it."

The blue eyes flickered briefly and a silence descended.

Hensley sucked on his cigarette.

Presently the outlaw told the medic, "Okay. But I couldn't trust my own mother, Doctor. I'll have to go in with you. And I have to keep you in sight at all times."

"Fair enough," Hensley murmured. He drew the

blood sample, took another look into the patient's eyes, and headed immediately for the door.

Bolan thrust the dark glasses at him. "Security," was all he said.

Hensley nodded and donned the glasses. He opened the door and felt his way to the ground, then waited for the guiding hand.

Twenty or so paces later—he'd lost interest in the count—the glasses were removed and he stepped on briskly without losing stride.

The two men entered the hospital side by side. They went straight to the deserted lab, and the tall man stood with that fine grace fully intact and watched while Hensley ran his tests.

Ten minutes later the quiet man with the interesting blue eyes murmured his thanks and accepted the written instructions and medicines which the doctor handed over.

Hensley brushed aside the show of gratitude with a wave of the hand, saying, "I'm going to report this, of course. But it's going to take me about another ten minutes to make up my mind that something is funny here, and then probably another five to find the telephone number for the police station. I don't know what you're all about, Mr. Bolan, but then neither do I know what I am all about. Good luck to you, sir."

The tall man grinned, the frostiness of those eyes melting to an incredible warmth.

He said, "Live large, Doctor," and spun away.

Hensley stopped him at the lab door with a quiet call. "Sergeant Bolan! There's a telephone number on

47

those instructions I gave you. It's an aid station, well clear of enemy fire. And the medic on duty *does* make house calls."

Another flash of friendly eyes and the phenomenon was gone.

Hensley was not at all surprised to find that his own death funk had vanished.

"What the hell have I done?" he wondered out loud.

He dropped onto a stool and gazed at his hands. Human hands, not Godly ones.

Who the hell ever said that medical doctors were supposed to be something a bit more than human?

But then, human hands and human thought could do quite a bit—yes, quite a bit. If any one wanted to know just how much, then they could ask the indomitable Sergeant Bolan about it.

The doctor picked up his bag, returned to the desk and signed back in, then went to take another look at that dying old woman in the cardiac ward.

5: THE ALLY

Bolan's "base camp" was a Holiday Inn on Interstate 20 in the stretch between Big Spring and Abilene. It had been established some days earlier, and from there Bolan had operated during the reconnaissance phase of the strike into Texas.

The disguised "war wagon," an Econoline van that had been dandied up with colors and decals of a fictitious oil company, returned to base camp on that spring morning at shortly after eight o'clock—just in time to evade a state trooper's checkpoint which at that very moment was being established along the exit from the interstate highway.

The motel lay within sight of the roadblock.

So, sure, Bolan had known that the girl would cost him. The cops were just reacting a bit quicker than had been anticipated.

He parked the van right at his door and went inside for a quick check-out of the room, then he wandered over to the lobby for a brief and casual recon of that area, then on to the coffee shop.

He bought a carry-out pot of coffee and a bag of Danish pastries and took them to the room. Then he brought the girl in, covered from head to toes and slung casually over a shoulder.

It was not likely that anyone had noticed that operation. There was very little life around the motel at that hour. Most of the early risers had departed; the others were still on their pillows or in the coffee shop; the maids had not yet begun to stir.

He put the girl to bed, hung a "Do Not Disturb" sign on the door, and moved the war wagon to an open spot on the back of the lot, to which he would have an unobstructed view from his room.

The doctor had assured him that the girl would be okay. The drug in her system was "a simple sedative." Bolan should allow her to "just sleep it off." The medicines provided were no more than high-potency vitamins and "something to combat a possible nausea."

The Executioner had no intention whatever of allowing Judith Klingman to "just sleep it off." There was no time for sleeping.

He returned to the room and stripped to his underwear. Then he wrapped a towel around the girl and cinched it in tight at her waist.

He carried her into the shower and held her beneath a spray which was several degrees below comfortable temperature, talked to her, and gently patted her face.

He took her out of there as soon as she began to stir and lay her on the carpeted floor, soaking wet. He worked on her, then, with the wet towel, vigorously rubbing and massaging from the soles of her feet upward, talking to her all the while in reassuring tones.

The girl was tingling red all over and beginning to quiver when he switched from wet to dry and started buffing her with a fresh towel. She came out of it fighting, arms and legs flailing, eyes as round as saucers and scared as hell.

He had a hand ready to shut off any screams, but the terrified girl had not yet found her voice, and Bolan's own gentle tones turned the trick.

"Stop that," he commanded, quietly but firmly. "Behave yourself. I'm not your enemy, Miss Klingman."

She fell back to the floor, chest heaving, relaxed in surrender but eyes still locked to his. "Wh-what're you doing?" she gasped in a hoarse whisper.

Bolan told her, "Trying to get you off your back and on your feet, believe it or not." He smiled and draped the towel lengthwise upon her body. "You've been out of it. I've just been trying to bring you back."

Sure, she was some kind of beauty. Don't even notice the long, beautifully tapered legs and flaring thighs, the creamy little mashed-potato belly and voluptuous quarterdeck. It was that Texas co-ed face with the deep-pool eyes that seized Bolan's emotions and made him aware of his own seminude condition.

He left her lying there and snared a towel for himself from the bathroom rack, knotted it about his waist, and went for a cigarette.

When next he checked she was sitting upright, the towel held in tight little fists just beneath her chin, giving him a frankly curious stare.

He asked, "How do you feel?"

"All over," she replied.

Bolan chuckled. "Hope I didn't wear away any skin. I, uh, had to . . ."

51

"Yes, I understand. Thank you."

It was a nice voice, intelligent, with it—despite the drug fuzzies. Very definitely Texan, pleasingly so.

He told her, "I have plenty of coffee. Some pastries, too, if you'd like. And if you're feeling a bit seasick, I even have something for that."

"Coffee sounds fine," she said.

Those eyes had not left him.

He found a couple of cups and poured the coffee; then he went to the bathroom and tossed her another towel. "Only thing I can offer in two-piece ensembles," he said. "Sorry, it's that or nothing."

She said, "I've had plenty of nothing."

Great. A sense of humor could be her greatest asset at the moment.

He turned his back to give her modesty a fighting chance but then had to whirl and grab her as she stumbled to her feet and pitched forward. He held her there, upright but swaying, and affixed the towels to her himself.

She smiled drunkenly and murmured, "Pretty much of a wasted effort by now, isn't it?"

Bolan said, "Believe me, it's not."

He led her to the dresser and anchored her there. "Stay on your feet," he advised. "The swimming will stop if you'll fight it through."

Her eyes were trying to focus on the black skin suit and the Beretta rig which Bolan had laid out on the bed. She said, "No dream."

"What?"

"I thought it was a dream. The black knight. No dream."

He understood, although not completely. "I pulled you out of the Wells," he explained, trying to fill in blanks for her.

"Yes. Thank you."

He held the coffee to her lips and she sipped it. Pretty soon she was gulping it, and then holding it for herself, watching him with luminous eyes above the rim of the cup.

He told her, "When the room stabilizes, you might try walking some."

"You're not a policemen, are you."

He shook his head. "I'm Mack Bolan."

"My gosh!" She set the cup down with a clatter and beat a staggering path to the bed, sat down, sprang right back up, and walked a circle of the room. "The wobblies are leaving," she announced.

Bolan told her, "You're pretty tough."

"So are you. I should have known—I *would* have known if I'd been in my right mind—I mean, the minute you came crashing in. I've been following your—your career almost from the start. You are quite a famous man, you know."

"Notorious," he replied, "is the word."

"No. Famous, too. Lots of people are rooting for you, Mr.—oh, no, this won't do, this mister and miss business. I mean, not with nothing but a couple of towels between us."

She was sounding giddy, and seemed to be having trouble with the focus of her eyes.

Bolan suggested, "Too much too fast, Miss Klingman. Cool it a little. Try some more coffee."

"But I can't call you Mack, can I? It just doesn't sound like a whole name."

"It's all I've ever had," he assured her. "Come on. Coffee time again."

She lurched toward the dresser. Bolan had to steady her while she went to work on the second cup.

Those eyes were working him over again, too. He grinned at her. She grinned back and grimly stuck with the coffee.

Between gulps she told him, "I feel honored."

He said, "Well, that makes us even."

"I kept expecting someone to rescue me. But my gosh. Look who came."

He asked, "How long were you there?"

"Oh, well, since—what day is this?"

Bolan told her.

The deep-pool eyes flattened out somewhat but then bounced back quickly. "Well, no wonder it seemed like forever," she said.

Bolan was digging this girl more and more by the minute.

"I guess it was about—well, a week ago. When they started jabbing the needles at me. I almost escaped. Daddy will be very proud of that. But *they* were furious. They took all my clothes away and locked me in. And started the march of the needles. Every time I'd start rising up out of the fuzzies, wham, another needle. I figured I was growing old and haggy in that darned room. Maybe I did." She craned her head toward the mirror, made a face at it, and said, "Yep. *Damn* them."

54

Bolan chuckled and told her, "You look great. Are you saying that you were held for only a week?"

"Oh, no. I've been out there since January. Under house arrest. Can you imagine? Right here in the United States of America? Right here in the heart of Texas? Something like that happening? I couldn't believe it. I just couldn't. And then I *had* to, because it just went on and on."

He asked, "Why were they holding you?"

"You don't know why?"

He replied, "No. I'm asking you."

Those eyes had gone just a trifle wary. She said, "Well, I don't know why."

Bolan said, "Baloney."

"Some people think that you're secretly working with the government," she said.

"I'm not."

"Some people think so. So I'd better just keep quiet. For now."

He told her, "You'd better not. Look, Miss Klingman, you're in a bad spot. The only reason you're alive right now is because the Mafia figured to gain something through the fact that you *are* alive. They—"

"The *Mafia!*" she gasped.

He blinked at her and said, "Who did you think? These people don't play silly games. They play for keeps. The mere fact that you are back into the world again could make you chief candidate for a hit."

The girl was still having trouble with that first

idea. "The Mafia?" Her eyes were round and horror-stricken.

It could not have been an act. Bolan knew it could not, especially considering the state of her drug-impacted mind.

He said, "I assumed you knew that much."

"What have they done to my father?"

"As of about twelve hours ago, your father was alive and well in Dallas."

"How do you know that?"

"It's my business to know," he told her. "But I need to know a lot more. And I need your help. I need your help, Miss Klingman, like the flowers need the sun."

She pushed the empty cup toward him. "Fill 'er up," she demanded—and Bolan knew that some deep dimension of this girl was beginning to respond to the heavy reality of her situation.

He said, "You will help me, won't you?"

"*Help* you," she said. "I'll carry you piggyback all the way to Dallas."

Bolan had no doubts whatever that she meant precisely what she said.

And she was about to get a chance to prove it.

The parking lot outside was suddenly filling with cops.

6: TRIPLE OPTION

Judith Klingman tumbled into the bed and pulled the sheet up to her chin, then whipped off her towels and fired them at Bolan. He relayed them to the bathroom and invested a few seconds of precious time on the girl's positioning.

The master of "role camouflage" knew that proper staging was all-important to the success of any illusion.

He stacked the pillows at her back and lifted her half-upright, then rearranged the covering sheet so that the top hem lay squarely across the ample bosom.

Finally he placed a Danish pastry in her hand, said, "Take a bite," and went immediately to the bathroom, taking skin suit and Beretta with him for concealment there.

He stepped into the shower and wet himself down, patted shaving lather on his face, draped a towel across his shoulders and cinched one about his waist, set the hot water tap of the basin to a slow trickle, and waited for the inevitable visitation at the front door.

He'd freshened the lather twice and Judith had choked down half of the Danish before the law presented itself.

Bolan slumped his shoulders into a rounded curl

and gave the girl a reassuring wink as he stepped past the bed to answer the summons.

She looked scared. He murmured, "Just cool it. Play it by ear, and off my cues."

She nodded.

He let the callers rap once more before he called through the closed door in a surly voice, "What? No maid, not now. See the sign?"

A respectful Texas drawl responded with, "Police, sir. Please open the door."

Bolan waited a couple of beats, then turned the latch and cracked the door to the limit of the chain travel.

"I didn't call any police," he muttered, peering through the crack. "How do I know . . . ?"

An eye met his through the opening, a troubled eye with apology and regret radiating from it, belonging to a diffident youth in a motel uniform.

"It's the sheriff's office, sir. I'm sorry. It's some sort of routine check. They'd appreciate your cooperation."

Bolan grunted and closed the door, released the chain lock, then opened wide and stepped back.

Cops with shotguns were prowling the parking area, peering into cars. The young clerk at Bolan's door was accompanied by two men in spit 'n' polish khaki and heavy leather, roll-brim Western hats and immaculate boots. The uniform shirts fairly blazed with impressive insignia and flap-pocket decorations. Both men were rather young and nearly as ill-at-ease as the clerk.

Bolan's reception of the invasion of privacy was a

skilled mixture of irritation and willingness to cooperate. "My wife's still in bed," he growled. "What's going on?"

The clerk was riffling a thin stack of registry cards.

One of the deputies told the Executioner: "We've had reports of a dangerous fugitive in the county, sir. We're checking out all the public places. Sorry for the inconvenience but—you know how these things go—we have to look."

Both officers had stepped across the threshold into the room. The clerk remained outside, nervously shuffling his cards.

Bolan mentally shook his head over their "procedure." They were blocking the doorway, framed in it, with all the light behind them, sitting ducks for any "dangerous fugitive" who might wish to blast his way out of that corner.

He snapped on the overhead lights and waved his arm in an invitational sweep of the premises. "Have at it," he said.

The official eyes had gone magnetically to the appealingly staged "bed scene" but did not linger there more than a split second.

One of the lawmen wandered through toward the bathroom, mumbling an eyes-averted apology to the lady in bed. The other was scrutinizing the motel card on which Bolan had registered his occupancy several days earlier.

"Name, sir?" he murmured.

Bolan replied, "Edwards. You want identification?"

"No, sir. Is that your Porsche parked just outside?"

"One-third mine, two-thirds the Cotton State Bank's."

The deputy grinned. "Yes sir. Do you happen to remember the license number?"

Bolan told him, then asked, "Didn't I put that on the card?"

"Yessir, just checking. Uh, you didn't register your wife, Mr. Edwards."

"Didn't I?" Bolan clucked his tongue. "Too long a bachelor, I guess. I keep forgetting."

"Yessir." The deputy shot a quick glance toward the bed. Judith was glowering at her half-devoured Danish, pouting.

The other officer returned from his hasty inspection of the steamy bathroom, snapped a sideways glance at Bolan, and went on outside.

The spokesman for the law said, "Sorry to trouble you, Mr. Edwards. We appreciate the cooperation." He made a little half-salute toward the bed. "Mrs. Edwards." He paused in the open doorway for another glance at the bed. "Uh, it's state law, sir. Each adult occupant is supposed to be registered by name."

Bolan smiled through the hardening shaving lather. "I'll stop by the office and fix it," he assured the young officer.

The guy touched his hat again and stepped outside.

Bolan closed the door and turned a smile toward the girl.

She released a long sigh and said, "Wow. Easy as pie. Just the same I'll take my suspense in the movies, thanks."

"It only seemed easy because it worked," Bolan

60

corrected her. "A false breath, one wrong word, and the roof would have fallen in. You did great. But the suspense has hardly begun."

Five minutes later he was fully dressed, the Beretta snug in her usual place of concealment beneath his left arm.

The girl remained as Bolan had placed her, nude beneath the thin sheet, propped onto the pillow, the half-eaten Danish in her hand, watching him with mounting curiosity.

"Yes, you're a mighty tough guy, Mack Bolan," she observed. "So sweet one minute and so—so *deadly* the next. I'll bet you're going out looking for blood, aren't you."

He said, "Something like that."

"What about me?" she asked in a little-girl voice.

"That's your option," he replied. "You're in no shape to travel and you're certainly not dressed for it. I don't know how far a couple of towels would get you. From where I stand, though, you have three choices. You can pick up that phone and call the law, tell them what's happened, demand protection. Or you can try to contact your father, expose yourself to the people who are holding him, and end up right back in their hands. Either way, even if you call the cops, you'll probably wind up right back where I came in."

"You said *three* choices," she murmured.

"The third is probably the toughest, maybe even the most dangerous. The third choice is me, Judith. You can tell me all you know. Then you can stay right where you are until I've had a chance to clear a place for you out there in that no-man's-land. But there's no assurance that I'll ever get back. And it has to be your decision, not mine."

She showed him a wan smile. "It's like I'm a quarterback. I have to call the play. No help from the bench."

Bolan nodded. "Third down. And it's your option. You can pass, keep, or hand off."

"Let's huddle and talk this over," she said solemnly.

"No way. It's a two-minute drill, third-and-ten situation. The play has already been called and I'm up front, in the pit. It's a sweep to the strong side, quarterback option."

"You're my right tackle," the girl murmured.

He said, "I see you understand the game."

"This is football country, Mack." She gave him a long, unblinking gaze, then sighed and added, "It's the one thing Daddy and I always had in common. Yes, I understand the damn game. But this isn't a game of football, is it."

Bolan said, "Very much the same. Call it."

She fluttered her eyelids and said, "You're going to pull and block for a strong-side sweep. I can follow my blocker or I can exercise my options."

"That's about it."

"But your assignment is fixed. Preordained. You go with or without me."

"Right."

Her eyes were brave but the voice just a bit trembly with the decision. "Okay. I'll keep."

He twirled a chair around and straddled it, gazing at the girl across folded hands. "Welcome aboard.

You've got about five minutes to tell me everything you know."

The telling was painful, often choking, sometimes teary—and it took quite a bit more than five minutes.

But when the Executioner stepped out of that motel room, he carried with him very clear directions to the front. He knew, within certain limits, the name of the Mafia game in Texas—and, no, it was not football. It was a game for keeps—for control, maybe, of the entire Western world.

Cosa di tutti Cosi—the Thing of All the Things—the *Cosa Nostra* master plan for world domination—was taking firm root in Texas soil.

And there were no options whatever for executioner Bolan.

7: SIGNALS

A couple of sheriff's deputies were still nosing around the motel. Bolan noted that the war wagon had drawn no more than passing interest, but he was not about to push his luck in that direction.

He climbed into his hot wheels, the Porsche, and eased out of there.

The roadblock across the interstate exit was still in place but having minimal effect on the flow of traffic. The troopers were spot-checking only, waving most cars on without even a full stop. The half-hearted effort told Bolan something about the state of alert in this particular area. The on-ramp was not being monitored at all.

It was a huge state, after all, and severely under-policed.

That could be both good and bad, depending upon the point of view. For Bolan, at this particular moment, it was good.

He smiled grimly at his own reflection in the car mirror and pulled in beside a phone booth at a service station just off the interstate. The long-distance operator connected into a Massachusetts area code and rang the number which Bolan supplied.

A familiar voice responded to the third ring. The operator announced, "Collect call from Mr. Al La Mancha. Will you accept charges?"

"You got the wrong number," came the expected reply. "I don't know any La Mancha."

The operator verified the number, apologized, disconnected, and asked Bolan, "Would you like to check that number, sir?"

He replied, "Sure. I'll call you back."

He wandered into the office of the service station, bought coffee from a coin-operated dispenser, small-talked the attendant, got a pocketful of change, and stepped back into the phone booth precisely five minutes after he'd left it.

This time he direct-dialed, fed in his coins, and waited for the ring at another booth two thousand miles away.

The same familiar voice was there, a bit breathless this time. "Yeah, damn it, hello."

"La Mancha here."

"I wasn't exactly expecting Alice in Wonderland," Leo Turrin told the Executioner.

Turrin was a Massachusetts family underboss—also an undercover federal cop and Mack Bolan's truest friend in the world.

Bolan was chuckling. He said, "Leo, you're getting soft. Or else that two-block walk gets a little longer every time."

"Yeah, you've hit it," Turrin replied sourly. "On both counts. I hope to God you're not calling from deep in the heart of Texas."

"How'd you guess?"

"Good Christ. It's true, then. Sarge, get the hell out of there!"

"No way, Leo. This is happy hunting grounds. These guys are—"

"I know, damn it, I know. Listen, Texas is so hot that I only started hearing the whispers a few weeks ago, myself. How the hell do you get onto that stuff? Brognola just turned his strike force into the problem ten days ago. All they're getting so far is odors."

Harold Brognola was an on-again, off-again Bolan ally—also a rather highly placed official in the U.S. Department of Justice. His special project was organized crime, and this circumstance had placed him on collision courses with Bolan's pathways during several of the campaigns.

Bolan said to Leo Turrin, "And all you're getting is whispers, eh?"

"Yeh. That's about par. Except right now all of a sudden I'm hearing some loud screams. The Bolan Bunch has been activated, and I hear—"

"Hold, hold. That's a new one. The Bolan Bunch?"

"The new headhunters. In your case, successors to the Taliferi. You should've been checking in with me. It's a new counterforce headed up by a guy named Lileo. They—"

"Never heard of that one," Bolan interrupted.

"One of the young Turks out of New Orleans," Turrin explained. "A real headman, I hear. Anyway, it's a nationwide outfit. Crews in all major cities. This Lileo calls the shots from his new headquarters in St. Louis. It's a network operation, Sarge—like a spider web. These crews are poised to converge on any point you touch. It's their only reason for living.

And right now, buddy, they are converging on Texas."

"It figures," Bolan commented. The humor had left his voice. It was grim, now—thoughtful. "Well, that's just one more factor. I'm not playing defense this time, Leo."

"You might have to."

Bolan was remembering his little speech to Judith Klingman about "a two-minute drill." He told his friend Turrin, "Just gives me less time for a score. I was playing on a couple more days' worth of numbers."

"No. No way, Sarge. If you must hit, then damn it hit and git. And I mean quick. Don't give these boys a chance to set up for you."

"I'll need some quick intelligence," Bolan said, and both men understood that it was an urgent request.

The troubled sigh from Massachusetts told it like it was. "You're in a top security area, Mack."

Bolan sighed and said, "Don't I know it. Leo—it's the Big Thing again, in spades. They're going for a Texas takeover."

"Takeover of what?"

"I just said it. Texas. The proverbial heart of it, at the least."

The undercover fed sent a nervous, coughing chuckle across the two thousand miles of telephone line. "Hell. That's quite an order, isn't it? The whole damned state of Texas?"

Bolan replied, "Just about. The politics, the economy, the whole bag."

"Then they must have gotten a lot smarter than anything I've seen yet. Since Lansky, anyway."

"This looks bigger than anything Lansky ever tried," Bolan told him. "It's a coalition—a gathering of brains, money, and muscle."

"Cannibal operation?"

"Yeah, but much more than that. International interests, even."

"Sounds very romantic," Turrin growled.

"Yeah, well, I lucked onto a small piece of it. I believe they're working several angles all at once. The piece I caught is oil."

"Is what?"

"Oil, the stuff that makes the world go 'round."

"What the hell!" Turrin snorted. "They can't hope to take over anything that big! Why that's—that's . . ."

"Yeah, ridiculous. That's exactly why it might work. I thought the same thing, at first. But you're liable to wake up some morning to find that you've got to play ball with the mob before you can gas your car or heat your home. Or open your factory or roll your trucks or whatever the hell you can think of that makes the world hum."

"Aw hell, Sarge."

"I know, Leo. It's hard to believe. But they are well into it. Already they've gobbled up at least one small independent, the Klingman outfit, and—"

"Hey! I've heard that one! Is that—what is that?"

"Just the beginning. I hope. I need you to tell me just how far the cancer has spread. Now listen and get it the first time around. I've got to get off center and start my sweep. Three months ago the small corporation known as Klingman Petro was rolling high in profits and you couldn't have bought a share of the stock with your own blood. At this moment the company is in collapse. You can't give the stock away except to people in the know, and then that's about what you have to do—give it away. Klingman has been gobbled up whole body by a so-called conglomerate that's chartered in Delaware under the name International Bankers Holding Corporation. I believe it's a mob front operation. But it's more than that, too. A well-known shiek or sultan or whatever from the Mideast is an officer in IBH— one of the invisible ones. I think the—"

"Hold it, Sarge. This is beginning to sound like something out of Arabian Nights. Do you know what the hell you're—?"

"I said to get it the first time around, Leo. My numbers are getting short. Believe it or don't, but damn it listen and take off from there when I've finished."

"Okay, okay," Turrin muttered.

"My informant couldn't recall this Arab's name, but I'm assured it's well known to the state department. He's some sort of a maverick over there—never has played ball with the Arab unity idea, and apparently he has ideas of his own. But he's picked himself some damn tough partners. He'll probably find himself in the cannibal's pot before it's over. The Italian mob and the French mob have a piece of the action, too, if the names of the IBH directors mean anything. There might also be some action coming in from the

Bahamas, so you might check that direction of interest."

"Mack, this is just too goddamned—okay, okay. Go on."

"That's about it. Except for one final item. My contact tells me that the wells of Klingman Petro are pumping at maximum flow, despite official reports to the contrary. I'd sure like to know where that crude is going, whether it's being stored or refined—and, if it is being refined, where. Klingman's refineries are all but shut down."

"Sarge, I don't know how the hell I can—"

"And I'd like to know what gives with their pipeline operation. Something damn peculiar is going on in that area. They're changing out pumping stations, rerouting feeders and trunk lines, all sorts of weird moves."

The Pittsfield underboss howled, "Shit, I don't know anything about that stuff!"

"Then it's time to broaden your mind. See what you can dig up for me, Leo."

"Oh, sure, that's easy. I'll just waltz down to New York and crash in on Augie Marinello. I'm sure he'll spill the whole thing to me. In a pig's ass!"

Bolan chuckled solemnly. "How is Augie? Last I saw or heard, he was being rushed away to the medics."

"He's alive, just. They took his legs off."

Bolan said, "I get no cheer from that. An old man should be able to die in one piece, even an old man like that one."

"There's, uh, quite a mystery about that, Sarge.

70

They say you gave 'em a white flag to carry the old man off."

"No mystery," Bolan clipped back. "It just seemed the thing to do. I did it."

"Yeah. Well . . ."

"Take care, Leo. Don't expose yourself."

"You're a hell of a guy to be handing out advice like that," Turrin replied. "Watch out for Lileo and the Bolan Bunch. It's a hard team."

Bolan said, "Yeah. How're things in Pittsfield?"

"Quiet as ever, since you left. Uh. Sarge. There's another guy in Texas you should know about."

"Quaso?"

"Okay, so you know already. He's out of the same mold as Lileo. And the old men love him. He'll be working hard to preserve that love."

Bolan said, "Yeah. Go to work, Leo."

He hung up, signalled the operator and settled the overtime charges, then direct-dialed a number in Dallas.

Barring any unforeseen problems, Jack Grimaldi should have had time to make it back to the Dallas base.

And it was time to sweep.

Right down Beloved Joe Quaso's throat!

8: NOT FOR LUNCH

The room was darkened. The only light was coming from the bed-mounted projector, a beam which splashed out in full color onto the smooth surface of the opposite wall upon which the two-dimensional likenesses of a man and a woman, both nude, moaned and gasped with the attentions each was receiving from the other.

A small, skinny man sat slumped in a chair near the circular bed, gazing with rapt interest at the activities unfolding upon the wall screen. Now and then he would snicker and shift restlessly in the chair.

A door opened and another man entered the room. He called, "Hey, Boots. Larry Awful wants you."

"Wait a minute," was the lazy response. "C'mere and watch this. This is terrible. I don't believe it."

The newcomer closed the door and spun a chair into position beside the other one. "Which one is this?" he grunted as he dropped into the chair.

"It's about this guy that comes home for lunch. He's hungry, see. But his old lady has got different ideas. She's hungry too, see, but not for lunch. She starts working him over right there in the kitchen. First thing you know she's pouring food all over him and licking it off, all kinds of food, see—even minestrone soup. Hey, lookit that! Ain't that terrible?

"All these guys in these movies are fags, Boots. Hell, he ain't getting a damned thing out of that."

"George, all you gotta do, just lay there. And enjoy it. Whattaya mean, queer? I'd do it."

"You'd let them take pictures of you doing it?"

"With a babe like that? You kidding? Just show me the place, man."

George scooted to the edge of his chair and said, "Come on. Larry wants you."

"It's just about another minute. Hey, he assigned me to the damn flick room, didn't he? Wait just a minute. It's the punch line you gotta see. See, this guy has been turned every way but loose by this broad, see. God, he's even turning green in the gills, I guess, and maybe he's going to throw up or something any minute. Finally he shoves her away and comes up on his elbow, see. And he says, 'Look, honey, I married you for better or for worse. But ...'

"She says, 'Yeah, okay, but what?'

"And he says—get this, this is the punch—he says, 'But *not* for *lunch*.' Ain't that rich?"

George rose half out of his chair then quickly dropped back.

He growled something in a half-strangled voice and a leg shot up as though responding to a knee-hammer reflex then returned to the floor with a thump. There were energetic hand movements, also, as though he was pounding the arms of the chair in a convulsive fit of hilarity.

Boots was cackling over the ribald humor and being fed further by the supposed appreciation of his partner. He leaned across the darkness to share

73

the moment eye to eye—then froze, an explosive cackle wrenching off at about chest level.

George's eyes were bugging almost out of his head and his tongue was hanging out, the body beginning to sag.

And then Boots saw the clenched fists poised above that lolling head, sensed the dark presence standing there behind that chair, *knew* that silent judgment had found him in a darkened bedroom in Texas.

He croaked, "Holy!" and tried to get some feet beneath him, to thaw frozen limbs, to send survival commands through numbed nervepaths.

But there was not that much time left in the universe for Boots Faringhetti.

Those clenched fists moved swiftly in a circular pattern above his own head, something soft as nylon and strong as steel became imbedded in the soft flesh of his throat, and the final sight on earth recorded by those bulging eyes was a male figure upon a darkened bedroom wall delivering the favored punch line: "But not for lunch."

The light on the wall flickered, the images vanished. The movie projector whirred into automatic rewind. A black shadow moved across the room, as silent as a sigh.

A door opened, bringing in a shaft of daylight and the head and shoulders of a youngish man in shirtsleeves and sideleather. He called into the darkness, "Will you guys for Christ's sake get it off! Boss'll be here any minute. Put that stuff away and don't leave no mess!"

The impressively long barrel of a pistol with an

74

ominous bulb at its muzzle end moved away from the wall and grafted itself to the man's forehead.

A quiet, no-nonsense voice warned, "Don't breathe. Step inside. Shut the door."

Yes. Judgment had come to Texas.

But not for lunch.

9: THE AWFUL TRUTH

Quaso stepped from the elevator and into the foyer of the penthouse, his two tagmen close on his heels. The front men of the palace guard scrambled to their feet, one of them reaching hastily to squelch the Nashville sound blaring from the transistor radio.

The Chief Enforcer growled, "What's with you boys? Don't you know there's a war on? Damn it, you keep alert!"

"Yessir. We were alert. We just—"

"Shut up! Keep alert!"

"Yessir."

Quaso swept on inside and immediately yelled, "Larry! Get in here!"

The tagmen exchanged nervous glances and drifted toward the kitchen.

A lanky middle-aged man with a hawkish face slouched into the room, a hand-rolled cigarette dangling from stained lips. "Yeah, boss," he said casually. "How'd the meeting go?"

Quaso yelled, "Larry, goddamn it, you look awful! You clean yourself up!"

It was a customary greeting. The rangy hardman just grinned and replied, "Sure, boss. I got an appointment for a manicure, first thing next week."

Quaso laughed, then sobered abruptly and told his crew boss: "The awful thing, Larry, is those two boys

76

out front. They're on their ass out there. They're going to be on their *knees* if I ever catch them like that again. You get out there and straighten them out."

There was a "thing" between these two men, a closeness which was masked by the startling contrast of appearances as well as the gruff—sometimes yelling—character of their personal exchanges.

Quaso was gruff with everyone. It was his nature and—with regard to his own boys—his right. But the open insults to Larry Stigni were above and beyond anything suffered by others in the Quaso cadre. And yet there was genuine affection there, on both sides. Stigni—dubbed "Larry Awful" as a result of the abuse—took the whole thing with good nature. But he could say things to Jaunty Joe Quaso that no others in the group dared say.

Rumor had it that Stigni was a blood relative. People in the mob love to gossip, however, especially about one another, and of course there were many other explanations whispered around concerning the "thing" between Quaso and his crew boss—most of it highly implausible, with no basis whatever.

Stigni himself was tough as nails, as cold a killer as had ever come along the Mafia trails. As for Quaso —sure, he was tough too. But he did have this problem with women. Sometimes he beat hell out of his women and kicked them out in the middle of the night. Beautiful women, the cream of the Texas prairies with whom most of the boys would gladly share a cordial bed for an entire night.

Nobody was actually *saying* that Jaunty Joe had a homosexual thing going with Larry Awful. But the gossipy possibility had served as a subject for quiet jokes—especially because of the physical appearance of Stigni. A better nickname for him would have been "Buzzard"—and it is surprising that no one had ever hung it on him. Mob people are big on descriptive nicknames, particularly the behind-the-back variety.

But the hardmen generally liked Stigni. He took up for them, acted as a buffer for Quaso's harshness, saw to their general needs and comforts.

And he did so in this instance. "I told the boys to don't look like they're standing at attention out there," he explained to the Chief. "Don't worry, they've got eyes and ears open. These are good boys you've got here, Joe."

"Yeah, yeah, I know," Quaso admitted, dismissing the entire incident in a characteristically sudden reversal of mood.

Larry Awful moved to the bar and mixed a drink for the boss. Quaso went to a small desk near the windows, produced a small notebook from his breast pocket, and opened it to the entries of the day. "We've got trouble, big trouble," he told his head man.

Stigni brought the drink, commented, "We've had it before, right?"—and craned his head for a look outside. Although the penthouse capped a twenty-story building, the highest structure in the area, the crew boss closed the drapes that were immediately behind Quaso and mildly scolded him, "Stay away from open windows, boss."

Jaunty Joe glanced toward the draped window and chuckled. "This guy is no superman, Larry," he

78

replied. "Anyway, we think he's out snooping around the prairies."

"You never know," Stigni muttered, unconvinced of either statement. "How'd the meeting go?"

"We're screwing it down. Everyone is cooperating. Our man in Austin is beating the drums for a mobilization of all the reserve cops. There'll be a badge behind every rock in the state before nightfall."

Larry Awful made an uncomfortable face and lit a fresh cigarette to cover the emotion. Such things had never been done in the "old mob." You could juice a cop, sure, that was part of the game. But you never hid behind one. You couldn't really trust them that much.

Quaso was saying, "And we're trying to backtrack the smart ass. I finally got the story out of Woofer and a pretty fair description of the plane he used. Our guy at the airport is trying to run it down. Checking all the flight plans and air traffic control razzmatazz. Meanwhile we want to stay plenty hard right here. Our smartass might get some big ideas and decide to storm the citadel. The general feeling is that he won't. We think he's just feinting, shadowboxing, trying to provoke a response that will give us away. We're not playing that game, I mean the Texas Plan isn't. I sent the alert to St. Loo. Lileo's bunch will be swarming all over, might be here already."

"That's what bothers me," Stigni quietly commented.

"Huh?"

"Well if we have a cop behind every rock and Lileo swarming, that sounds like plenty of trouble right there. Besides, I don't trust Lileo."

Quaso laughed and took a stiff pull at his drink. "You're right, he's a smartass, himself. As for the cops, that's Lileo's problem. Let him worry about it, eh?"

"We're not going after Bolan ourselves? He hit our territory, boss."

"Our job is to stay hard and run the shop. That's our job, Larry. That's *your* job. Let the battlefield specialists handle the open warfare."

Larry Awful was not liking that decision, not even a little bit, but only his face was revealing the secret. Quaso caught the look, though, and jeered at it. "Hey, you want to be a big hero, Larry? You want to take a whack at big bad Bolan's head? Christ, he could *smell* you a hundred yards away. You haven't taken a goddamn bath since—"

That particular insult was aborted by a muffled explosion that vibrated the desk and sent Quaso's drink sloshing against the sides of the glass. Several paintings on the far wall tumbled to the floor and a chandelier started swaying.

Quaso's eyes popped wide as his head jerked toward the sound. He yelled, "What the hell?"

"Your cunt castle!" Stigni yelped, and took off running toward the master bedroom.

The lanky crew boss was halfway across the room and calling for reinforcements before the stunned Quaso could get his legs under him. Stigni hit the bedroom door at full gallop and bounced off.

The two tagmen had come running in from the kitchen.

By the time Quaso was up and moving, the other three were assaulting the door in a concerted attack.

It gave way just as Quaso reached the scene, Stigni and the tagmen lunging through the opening and brandishing hardware.

From that moment on, it seemed to Quaso as though he were watching a slow-motion scene on television, although actually the entire stunning thing spanned no more than a few seconds.

In the foreground were his three boys—wheeling in half-frozen movements (it seemed)—off balance, half falling—trying to get set to handle that sense-boggling scene opening to them.

In the near background were the three housemen, two of them sprawled in chairs, eyes bugging in death, garroted—the third lying face down in a pool of fast-spilt blood.

Worst of all was back there at the windows, the big guy in the black combat rig, a big ugly silencer-tipped pistol at full extension and chugging death straight at Jaunty Joe Quaso.

The frames of action seemed frozen in that immovable moment.

Larry Awful, spinning on around in a continuation of the same motion that had catapulted him into that room and which was now sling-shotting him back outside—a terrible, bubbling hole flinging blood from the base of his buzzard nose—and Larry had never looked so awful.

The other two boys—going down in a tumble together, dying together as they had lived together, in lockstep, their weapons firing in a frantic but useless final discharge into the floor.

And then the moment moved on. The door swung back to close with a gentle click.

Quaso had not even gone for his gun.

He did so now, flinging himself to the floor and rolling out of that death alignment as slugs began punching through the closed door and sizzling the air above his head. He grabbed Stigni's foot and dragged him clear, also.

One of the boys from the foyer ran in, bug-eyed and yelling, "Boss! Boss!"

Quaso screamed, "Hit the alarm! Bolan's in there! Seal it off, close this goddamn building up tight!"

The front man did a fast pivot and raced back out.

Quaso steadied his revolver on the arm of an over-turned chair and aligned the sights with the bedroom door.

He muttered to his dear, dead friend, his punching bag since childhood, "Don't know how the smartass got in there, Larry. But he's sure as hell not walking out."

And then Quaso remembered the explosion.

The safe! The bastard had blown his safe!

Oh, Christ!

Now, for damned sure, Quaso could not allow the smartass to leave that room alive.

"Alert!" he screamed to the deserted penthouse. *"Full alert! Everybody!"*

For the first time in his life, Joe Quaso was totally alone.

And it was awful.

10: DEATH IN THE AFTERNOON

Bolan had dispatched the third houseman during that early, "silent phase" inside the enemy headshed. He had locked the door and opened the drapes at the wraparound windows to let some light into the problem, then began his search for hot intelligence—along the way spreading acid upon tape recordings, film cartridges, anything and everything that would offer no direct assistance to his Texas hit. He would have preferred to torch the joint, but a fire was utterly out of the question. Perhaps as many as a hundred families lived in the building; he could not gamble that the flames would not race out of control and punish the innocent along with the guilty.

As things turned out, it was a short search. The wall safe had been concealed with very little imagination. It was set into a panel in the walk-in closet, behind an array of hand-tailored suits.

It was during moments like this that Bolan remembered and thanked his deceased fellow death-squadroneer, Boom-Boom Hoffower. The munitions expert had shown the Executioner some interesting tricks with simple explosives, including the technique for opening things such as locked safes without destroying the contents in the process.

Bolan carefully worked in a thin strip of plastics, gently feeding the goop with fingertips into critical cracks and grooves. Then he set the detonator, stepped out and shut the closet door and stood clear.

There would be one hell of a hue and cry in response to that blast. The numbers would be very close. Too close, really, but he had not felt that he had a choice in the matter. *All* the numbers were going to be falling close during this campaign.

It was a good blow, not too much and not too little, with the right pressure in the proper places. The safe held ten packets of $100-bills—a tidy sum, probably clout money—also a stack of small notebooks and a four-by-six leather-bound ledger. The money itself was nothing but cream to the job—which was intelligence, not robbery. He scooped the entire contents into his chest pouch, wasting no time on inspection and evaluation of the yield.

Bolan was crossing to the windows when the reaction came—the assault upon the bedroom door. The closure jamb splintered, the door shuddered inward.

He was standing at the open window and waiting for them when they came tumbling in—and, at this range, the Beretta Belle could pick the legs off a fly.

He punched three cool whistlers into that human traffic jam at the door and saw it dissolving—saw also the stunned, frightened man standing rooted in his tracks just beyond the doorway.

The door was equipped with an automatic closing device. The first guy in had been spun completely around by a parabellum shocker between the eyes and flung back into the main room. The other two went down in a tangle of limbs, spinning off to the side, weapons blasting reflexively.

The door swung shut before Bolan could get off a round at the guy outside—Quaso, probably, although Bolan could not confirm that. There had been no more than a momentary meeting of eyes, and Bolan had never seen Quaso in the flesh.

He emptied his clip into the closed door to discourage further adventures on that front, then quickly ejected and fed in the reload as he went out the window.

It was a tight ledge, hardly more than a foot wide —but it had gotten him in, it would get him back out. He made his way to the corner where the nylon line awaited him, and went hand over hand to the roof.

From there the daring man in black went even higher, to the top of the air-conditioning tower, and there he set off a colored smoke marker.

Seconds later a helicopter swooped down in a crabbing dive from high altitude to hover briefly above the building. Bolan stepped onto a rope ladder dangling from the bird; then man and machine went straight up like an elevator.

A moment later they were in level flight toward open country. Bolan was inside and rubbing chafed hands; Jack Grimaldi was grinning like a Cheshire cat.

"God that was slick!" the pilot crowed. "Did you make contact?"

For reply, Bolan opened the chest pouch and slapped out several packets of the appropriated Mafia black money.

"I guess you did," Grimaldi commented, his eyes trying to estimate the value of the packets. Following a moment of silence, he asked the big man, "Cat got your tongue?"

Bolan replied, "Call it fear. Give me a minute."

"Sure." Grimaldi understood. Only a lunatic could live this guy's life and not know fear. The guy *looked* cold and hard and fearless. Inside, though, he was like any sane man. He was human.

At the moment, the entirely human blitz artist was siphoning off his nerves into an inspection of a leather-bound ledger.

Grimaldi asked, "The blackbook?"

Bolan growled, "Yeah. And very interesting."

"Any surprises?"

Bolan nodded. "A few. But also a lot of confirmation."

"What kind of confirmation?"

"Target confirmation."

The pilot raised an eyebrow and returned full attention to the task of aircraft control. It did not bother his feelings that Bolan did not confide everything in him. Mack Bolan was not an overly talkative guy in the first place. Which was fine. The less Grimaldi knew, the less he could be damned for. He didn't really wish to know anything. Bolan would tell him what Bolan thought he needed to know, and he'd tell him when he needed to know it. And, sure, that was fine.

"Can you get a fast plane?" the man in black asked, sort of offhandedly.

"How fast?"

"Fast enough to range me across this entire state in a single afternoon, with stops here and there. Then back to Dallas by nightfall."

"God. I don't know, Sarge. This is a big state. It would take something like a jet fighter. I don't know how the hell I could get hands on something like that."

"Can you fly one?"

"Has it got wings?"

Bolan chuckled, but it was not exactly a sound of mirth. "Doesn't the military ever surplus-off their old jets?"

"Well . . . yeah. Are you serious?"

A flash of blue ice assured Grimaldi that the Executioner was indeed serious.

"Well, yeah. There's an outfit right here in the area that refurbishes surplused war planes. Sells them to small nations. No armaments, though. They're stripped. Even so, I would have to grease a palm, probably, to get one on such short notice."

"Okay. Money's no problem, you know that. The war chest is bulging. Use what you need."

"What, uh—what's the idea?"

"The idea," Bolan replied with a chilling sigh, "is that I need to execute three men this afternoon. One in Austin. One in El Paso. One in Houston. They're big men. I'm hoping for a shock-wave effect. I want to rattle some teeth in this state."

"All in one afternoon?"

"That's the idea, Jack."

Sure. Okay. Grimaldi would get him the hot wings. And sure he understood "the idea." It was psychological warfare. Death in the afternoon. At three widely scattered points, all from the same guy. Sure. Bolan intended to cram their omnipotence right down their greedy throats.

"I'll find you a plane, soldier," Grimaldi said.

Bolan smiled, the gaze softening momentarily then hardening again into a grim contemplation of things ahead. "I was afraid you were going to say that," he muttered.

"It's going to be rough, eh?"

"Double rough. These big men, Jack. You have a right to know. They are not regular mob people."

"But involved."

"Up to their ears. Makes it all the worse. More scary. Respected people are very dangerous people when they go bad. And these guys have gone all-the-way rotten. I have to take them out."

"Okay." Grimaldi shrugged and looked away from those hard eyes. "You're the doctor, the surgeon. If they're all that big, though—well, I guess you know. There'll be howls and rage in very high places. Things are liable to get very hot."

"So what's new?" was the icy response.

Sure. Sure. Some guys *had* to damn themselves.

And, yeah, without guys like this, the world itself would be damned.

Jaunty Joe Quaso was not feeling particularly jaunty at the moment. He was, in fact, in the dying stages of a screaming fit.

"What the hell you mean, he got away?" he yelled at the discomfited hardmen. "Don't tell me the guy just materialized in my bedroom, hit my safe, poured acid on everything in the God damn place, knocked off half of my house force, and then just goddamn it dematerialized. He's got to be around here some place. He's playing you boys for suckers. Rip out the goddamn walls if you have to, but find that smartass! If that guy walks out of here with my stuff, I swear I'll see every one of you on the carpet. In front of the council itself, I swear. I'll run your lead asses clear out of the country!"

A stocky man who had been assigned to the ground-level lobby cleared his throat with a noisy gargle and told the boss, "I think you're right, Mr. Quaso. Nothing got by me. Not coming in or going out. I was right on that door every minute, I swear."

"Shut up!" Quaso stormed.

"Yessir."

"Get in there and shake down that bedroom again!" The command was given to no one in particular. None moved.

"He even killed Larry Awful! He killed your own boss, your own *amici!* You going to let him get away with *that* shit?"

Someone said, "We're going to miss Larry, Mr. Quaso. And the other boys, too. But we're not going to find that guy around here now. He's gone, sir, long gone. Probably out the window, that's the only way."

"You want to show me how?" Quaso yelled. "You want to demonstrate that little trick for me, Tucker? You want to walk that ledge? Or try climbing down the face of this building? You want to try that?"

The hardman dropped his eyes to the floor and muttered, "I'm not saying just anybody could do it, Mr. Quaso. But *that* guy . . ."

Silence descended, a silence in which every sigh, every grinding of teeth and shuffling of feet became magnified, oppressively so.

The bedeviled Texas Chief had apparently accepted the unacceptable. He began pacing energetically, as though trying to walk off his frustration, hands clasped behind his back, for all the world a Little Caesar with a truth too terrible to be borne.

The remains of his decimated personal cadre stood in awkward attendance, exchanging troubled gazes and awaiting the next round of bossly hysterics.

The telephone rang, and it seemed a welcome interruption of the deepening pall in that apartment. Several of the hardmen moved to answer the ring. The successful one scooped up the instrument and announced, "Yeah, penthouse."

He listened for a moment, said, "Just a second," and lifted his gaze to the expectant eyes of Jolted Joe Quaso. "Mr. Lileo is at the airport," he announced. "They're getting cars. Coming here, unless you have another suggestion."

The news was a magic wand waved above Quaso's troubled head. His mood immediately reversed. He rubbed his palms together and chortled, "Tell them to get here as quick as they can."

The hardman relayed the "suggestion" and hung up.

Quaso said, "You boys get yourselves a drink. Settle your nerves. Then back to your stations. Not you,

Tugboat. You've got the clean-up detail. You've got to stash these bodies somewhere."

"Even, uh, Mr. Stigni?"

"Yeah. Even him. Put them on ice somewhere. We'll see them properly buried when the fur has stopped flying around here."

And the fur would stop very soon, Quaso silently promised himself.

Poor Larry. He even died awful.

But so would someone else. Today, probably. Maybe even this afternoon, a certain someone else was going to die.

Very slowly.

11: THRICE DAMNED

At one o'clock in the afternoon on the day of the storm across Texas, a demilitarized jet fighter with undistinguished gray paint landed at the El Paso International Airport. It bore no markings of civil registry and had no radio. On the fuselage below the tandem cockpit was affixed a magnetic decal which read:

AmeriJet Inc.
Ferry Flight Service

The pilot was preceded from the cockpit by a tall man in clean white service coveralls which bore also a pocket decal identifying "AmeriJet Inc."

While the pilot shop-talked with the airport service attendant, the other man went to the base operator's terminal and claimed a rental automobile which had been reserved by telephone and was awaiting his arival. The rental applicant identified himself as "B. Macklin" and posted a cash deposit in lieu of credit credentials. He requested and received a map of the city and left the airport in a new Chevrolet Impala. The "time out" as recorded on the rental agency's record was 1:05 P.M.

At approximately a quarter after one, a new Chevrolet Impala pulled into the circular drive at the home of Brigadier General Nathan R. Spellman, USA (Retired). A tall man wearing white, unmarked coveralls interrupted the general at his lunch, on the patio, and was received with apparent good humor by the retired army officer after the caller identified himself as being "sent by Quaso."

It had been a "working lunch" for Spellman. He was dictating some business correspondence to a male secretary, whom he introduced as "my orderly."

The "orderly" was excused but was still within ear-shot when the tall man told his employer, "You've earned another medal, General."

Curiosity overcame discretion and the secretary looked back to see what the caller had meant by "another medal." The tone of the man's words, or something, had created the impression that some sort of presentation was being made.

According to this eyewitness account, General Spellman was holding something in the palm of his hand and staring at it "as though this man had handed him a rattlesnake."

At this point, the tall man in white coveralls said to Spellman, "As one soldier to another, General, I'm sorry about this."

He produced a black pistol, fired a single shot, and walked stonily past the dumbfounded secretary, returned to his automobile, and departed.

The general had been drilled squarely between the eyes. Death was instantaneous.

The rental car was checked in at the airport at 1:30.

According to the records at El Paso Tower, an aircraft without radio was cleared by telephone for takeoff at 1:35. The tower's logs identified the craft only as "AmeriJet Ferry 1." A later investigation failed to turn up any aircraft company called "Ameri-Jet Inc."

There was little official doubt, however, that "AmeriJet Ferry 1" had been used as a vehicle by Mack Bolan, the man called The Executioner.

Brigadier General Nathan R. Spellman, USA (Retired), died with a military marksman's medal clutched in his fist.

Spellman, who had retired from active duty two years earlier at the age of fifty-four, had been an intelligence officer in the army. He had distinguished himself in the field of electronic counterintelligence.

The general had lately been employed as special security coordinator for Klingman Petro, an independent Texas oil company. He was also listed as a "special consultant" to several state investigative agencies, including the security office for the State Capitol in Austin. He had been active in undisclosed activities associated with the Texas National Guard.

Later investigation also revealed a connection between Spellman and Gerald Whitson, a respected "international financier" with headquarters in Houston. Whitson controlled several Texas-based firms including a brokerage house which specialized in oil investments. He was forty-seven years of age, many times a millionaire, one of the postwar whiz kids who made it big during the state's industrial boom following World War II.

Whitson kept personal offices in one of Houston's new downtown building complexes. He was a bachelor. His office suite included sleep-in and eat-in facilities and was adjacent to a men's athletic club where he habitually put in one full hour each day in a rigid schedule of fitness exercises.

It was less than two hours after the "execution" in El Paso of General Spellman when a tall, clear-eyed young man presented himself at the Whitson suite in Houston, at the opposite side of the state. He was wearing slacks and jacket in "well-coordinated shades of blue," navy blue shirt, white tie. The caller presented "verbal identification" to the receptionist who passed the information to Whitson himself.

The man was admitted immediately and directed to "the lounge"—Whitson's on-premises apartment.

The financier was on a massage table, receiving a postexercise rubdown from an ex-boxer known as Wildcat McQueen.

As reported by McQueen, the "flashy dresser" perched himself atop a stool next to the massage table and the following conversation took place:

WHITSON: Getting a bit warm in Dallas?
STRANGER: You might say that. Other places too, we think.
WHITSON: That why they sent you down? To hold my hand?
STRANGER: Something like that.
WHITSON: Well forget it. I can take care of myself. Besides, you're too obvious, man, just too damned obvious.
STRANGER: Whatever you say. But you ought to know. Spellman is dead.

95

WHITSON: (alarmed) No! When?

STRANGER: Couple hours ago.

WHITSON: Okay, cool it, cool it. You about done, Wildcat? Wrap it up, eh. Wait—there's a catch under my arm here—the pectoral, I guess. Work that out first. (to the stranger) Uh, heart attack, eh? Spellman?

STRANGER: Something like that. It could happen to you.

WHITSON: No way. I'm as fit as a twenty-year-old. Right, Wildcat?

STRANGER: Not fit enough, Whitson.

WHITSON: What?

STRANGER: You didn't stay fit to live.

Whereupon the tall stranger in coordinated blue pressed a small metallic object into the financier's hand.

Whitson was lying stomach down on the table, his upper trunk raised and supported by his forearms, transfixed by the object in his hand.

He groaned, "Oh God! Wait a minute, now—*wait!* We can talk this out!"

McQueen instinctively stepped away from the table. The other man said, "Too late for talk, Whitson."

He drew a black pistol from inside his jacket and shot the financier once, directly between the eyes.

Then he told Wildcat McQueen, "Don't waste a medic's time. Just call the cops."

The man walked calmly out.

The first police unit arrived on the scene within minutes and promptly sealed the building. The only man to be seen leaving the building in the preceding few minutes was wearing white coveralls. But the "flashy dresser" was never again seen in Houston.

It was later learned that Gerald Whitson was listed as a director of the Delaware corporation known as International Bankers Holding. He was a member of the Oilmen's Club, a national advisor on petroleum export-import policies, and a behind-the-scenes power in Texas politics.

Whitson was also a partner in an Austin firm known as Oilfield Research and Conservation, a registered lobby with influential furrows in both the Texas Legislature and the US Congress.

And Gerald Whitson died with a marksman's medal in his hand.

No more than an hour following the killing in Houston, a man walked into the Austin office of Oilfield Research and Conservation and asked to see the prominent Texas attorney who ran that office.

The name of Joseph Quaso was passed as a means of identification and admittance.

Thomas Kilcannon, Esq., came to the door of his office to personally escort the caller inside.

Less than a minute later the man departed, letting himself out and nodding stonily to the secretary in the outer office.

"Don't go in there," he cautioned her. "Just call the cops. Tell them a man has been killed."

The secretary "called the cops" but did not follow the other advice.

She found Thomas Kilcannon slumped over his

desk in a pool of blood, his lifeless fingers resting upon a military marksman's medal.

A full police alert was ordered throughout the state of Texas at five o'clock, and "watches" were set up in the neighboring states of Arkansas, Louisiana, Oklahoma, and New Mexico. A special alert was flashed to the US Border Patrol.

Mack Bolan, the man at the top of the FBI list, was now positively known to be blitzing across the Lone Star State and evidently running amuck.

His latest three victims were all highly respected and influential citizens with spotless reputations.

In the eyes of certain Texas lawmen and in the words of one of that state's television newsmen, "Mack Bolan has made a tragic blunder. In trying to set himself up as judge, jury, and executioner, he has emerged in Texas as just another wild gunman with a lust to kill."

But, in Mack Bolan's personal journal, an entry of that same date reads: "I am neither judge nor jury. By their own actions they condemned themselves. This is war, and there is no such thing as morality in warfare. Let the world damn me. I did what had to be done."

The "world" had thrice damned Mack Bolan in Texas.

It was Oscar Wilde who wrote: "For he who lives more lives than one, more deaths than one must die."

But how many damnations could a human soul endure?

12: EYE OF TEXAS

"No flow, Sarge," Leo Turrin reported, his voice bursting with restrained emotion across the long-distance connection. "Nobody is talking about Texas, I mean not a word, not on either side of the fence. The mob guys change the subject quick at the very mention of Texas. The federal boys shake their heads and pass the buck along. I did make contact with Hal Brognola, though, finally. All he would say is that you are in a quote very sensitive area unquote. He's asking you to lay off. I get it there's a very up-tight investigation in progress down there, maybe been going on for some time. Anyway, he wants you to cool it."

"I can't cool it," Bolan replied. "And you can tell Brognola for me that his quote investigation unquote is long dead on the vine. It never got off the ground."

"Do you have proof of that?"

"I do. I can give him names and the precise market value of each one, if he's interested."

"You know he is," Turrin said wearily. His tone said that it was tough being a middleman between these two.

"Yeah, well, I'll get the intel to him—for whatever good it will do him. One of his own superiors is involved. Things are not exactly peachy-creamy in Washington these days, Leo. What the hell happened to official integrity in this country? The buying and selling of people seems to be the chief government activity."

"Hey, it's not all that bad."

"Isn't it? Listen, Leo, the biggest problem I have anymore is trying to separate the sheep from the wolves. They all look alike these days. They all smell alike. And they all act alike. I'm getting sick to my chin."

"God! Are you down!"

"Yeah. It's the company I keep. It's not just politicians and bureaucrats. Hell it's—Leo, I executed General Spellman today."

"Who?"

"Nat Spellman. He used to be counterintelligence chief for Europe. Then there was this big-shot financier who called kings and presidents by their first names. And a past officer of the Texas Bar Association who has autographed pictures of supreme court justices adorning his walls. I hung the mark of the beast on all three of them today, and in each case it was an award long overdue."

There was a long, heavy silence before Turrin replied, "Then that's what it's about."

"What?"

"Brognola is on his way to Texas with a large force of US marshals. Special government planeload."

"When were you talking to Hal?" Bolan asked.

"About an hour ago."

"That's probably it, then. I expected to make a lot of waves. No great surprise, Leo."

"Are you sure, uh . . . ?"

"About the targets? As sure as I've ever been."

"Yeah. Well. I hope you know what you're doing."

"So do I," Bolan told his friend in Pittsfield.

"Brognola knows we're in touch. He says to tell you he hopes you're out of the state by the time he gets there. You know what his assignment is, Sarge."

Bolan sighed. "Sure, I know."

"He says, just in case you are still around, he'd like a chance to parley with you before the deadline hostilities begin."

"Is he headed for Dallas?"

"Yeah."

"Okay. If you make contact in the next few hours, tell him to be on the sidewalk in front of the Federal Building at eight o'clock, main entrance, alone. I'll contact him there."

"Okay. Mack. Be careful."

"Sure. Everything all right there?"

Turrin understood the particular phraseology of that query. It had to do with Valentina Querente, Bolan's lady love, and the kid brother, Johnny Bolan. Turrin was keeping them in protective concealment. Bolan had not referred to the two by name since the near-tragic incident in Boston.

Turrin told the one-man army, "They're fine, but worried. She says you're getting too chancy."

Bolan growled, "I'm a dead man the minute I get too cautious. Watch the home fires, Leo."

"You know it. Oh. Do you still need the info about the oil fields?"

"I need everything I can find," Bolan assured him.

"Well I couldn't get much. But a guy in the Interior Department tells me about a new pipeline outfit that started down there a few months back. It's called Pecos Conduit, Inc. Couldn't find out what they're doing or where, but there's a definite link to your people. The Small and Poors has them listed as a subsidiary of International Bankers Holding."

Bolan said, "Bingo. Okay, thanks. It could mean something Ringing off, Leo."

"Wait a minute. Lileo's in Dallas with his whole bunch. You did some kind of job on Joe Quaso. No one is saying much about it, but it's for sure that Jaunty Joe is in some kind of disgrace at the moment. Lileo has been given full authority in Texas. He'll be waiting for your head to drop into his basket, Sarge."

"Know much about his operation?"

"No. But he's young, cagey, quick. I'd say dangerous as hell."

"Okay, thanks. I'll watch it."

Bolan hung up and stepped out of the phone booth.

A very nervous hotwing pilot awaited him. "What now?" Grimaldi asked.

"Now you return to base," Bolan replied. "I'll contact you."

"Where, uh, are you headed now?"

"Into town. I need a talk with a certain hotshot and I need to rattle some more teeth."

"What about the jet?"

"Leave it sit. Don't go near it."

"You know how much you *paid* for that thing?" Grimaldi asked, obviously pained.

102

Bolan smiled tightly and replied, "You know how much more it will cost if it gets tied to your tail?"

The pilot sighed. "See what you mean. Well, it's just money. What's money, eh?"

"It's just the stuff that buys men's souls," the Executioner mused. "Lay low, Jack. Stay out of sight."

"I know the routine."

As though in afterthought, Bolan said, "One quiet job you can do for me." He handed his one-man auxiliary a matchbook. "Call this motel. Use a pay phone. Ask for room one fifteen. If a man answers, hang up. If a woman, tell her to sit tight and cool it. Things are working."

Grimaldi smiled sourly. "I could go over and hold her hand."

"Forget it. It could be the last one you ever held."

"You, uh, think maybe . . . ?"

"We never know, do we?" Bolan replied. "Just handle it the way I told you, Jack."

"Count on that. Christ, man, watch yourself. I've been listening to the radio. The heat is on and pressures are rising."

Bolan grinned. "Like I said, Jack, things are working."

The two men shook hands and went separate ways—Grimaldi to his rotary wings and a quick return to sanctuary—Bolan to his hot wheels and an immediate return to the hell grounds.

The storm over Texas was gathering forces and this iceman was moving through the eye of it.

Very soon, now, that eye would close, thunder

and lightning would walk the plains, and the war for the soul of a great state would rage throughout the land.

The Executioner was moving in for the kill.

13: ROUSTED

Lileo stood several inches taller than the Chief Enforcer of Texas. He was broad of shoulder and nipped of waist, wore his hair in the new full look—could have stepped straight from the pages of *Playboy* or *Penthouse*. A handsome man—explosive, vigorous—he was quick to laugh and quick to snarl, self-assured, almost cocky.

Joe Quaso hated him.

The two bosses were bent over a large map of Texas which was spread across Quaso's desk, discussing in quiet tones their strategy for the night.

The apartment was aswarm with hardmen, some roaming restlessly from room to room while others gathered in sullen clumps and talked of minor things or gazed vacantly into one of the five television sets in the apartment. These were tough boys, recruited with the greatest discrimination from the various jungles of the nation. Many were combat veterans of Vietnam. All were young, hard, hungry.

New groups were arriving almost hourly, and the man-loading of the penthouse was reaching its outer limit. The glass doors to the garden terrace had been opened and that area also was brimming with bored, restless young men from around the country.

Two of Quaso's housemen were retelling for the umpteenth time the adventures of the morning, for the benefit of those in the Bolan Bunch who had just arrived from Florida. The story had grown with each recital, with the effect that the archopponent was now being credited with near supernatural powers.

Afternoon was blending into evening and a spectacular Texas sunset had turned the skies to red fires when a harried houseman, who had been kept busy passing out sandwiches and beer, approached the desk where the two bosses labored and announced that Mack Bolan was "on the telephone" and asking to speak to Mr. Lileo.

Quaso told his houseman to shut up and get lost and take his lousy jokes elsewhere, but the man insisted, "No sir, I think it's really him, I think it's the guy."

The two bosses exchanged glances. Lileo's eyebrows raised. He said, "Well, let's find out."

The houseman punched a button and shoved the desk phone over. Lileo winked at Quaso, picked up the instrument, and said, "This is Lileo."

A voice of cold steel told him, "Do a standard right face so I can get a good look at you."

Lileo chuckled and replied, "What, you're looking right through telephones too, eh? How do I know this is Bolan?"

"It's me," the voice assured him. "But I'm not looking at you through the phone, Lileo. I'm looking through a twenty-power. It's mounted on a four-sixty Weatherby. The back of your head is centered in the hairs and you're just about an inch below pointblank for this piece, which means you'd get it just above the vertebrae. But I've heard you have a pretty face, and I'd like to see it once before I mess it up forever. Right face, please."

The Chief of the Bolan Bunch laughed again but this time it sounded a bit hollow. He said, "This is childish, guy. You're not spooking anyone."

"That's not the intent. There, that's great. You have a good, strong profile. Now do it again so I can check the color of your eyes."

Lileo's hand closed over the mouthpiece. He snarled, "Check this joint out! You find a guy playing games with a telephone, bring me his head!"

The houseman had brought another telephone for Quaso.

A hush spread from the desk outward like ripples in a pool, engulfing the penthouse in a tense silence as the word spread that "something is up."

Grim-faced young men jostled their way through the crowds, searching for only what instincts could recognize or explain.

Quaso had a receiver to his ear and the voice was saying, "You crashing the party, Quaso? Move a little closer and I'll have you both in a tight two-shot."

Quaso took an uneasy step backwards.

"What the hell are you trying to pull off, guy?" Lileo asked, his voice vibrating with tension. He was gazing angrily out into space now, through the glass window and toward the nothingness of suburban Dallas at twenty stories up.

"There, now you have it," the cold voice told him. "You're looking right at me."

"Keep him talking," Quaso whispered urgently.

"I'm looking at nothing but another building about half a mile away," Lileo said into the phone. He said it casually, but the eyes were searching that distance out there, a gap of open space reddened by the setting sun.

"That's me," the dirty bastard said. "On the roof. But it's a little more than a half-mile. My range finder calibrates it at just a bit over nine hundred meters. Like I said, that's about an inch of trajectory-drop for the Weatherby. You'd like this piece, Lileo. Say the word and I'll show you how good it is."

Quaso cupped his phone and screamed, "Hit those drapes! Close 'em, damn it! Close the drapes!"

The guy was still talking. "I could have taken you, Lileo, at any time during the past ten minutes. You'd have never known what hit you. And they'd be cleaning your skull off that wall forever. But I'm saving you, for now."

"I think you're full of shit, guy," Lileo told him —but he was crouching now, sighing and obviously relieved that someone had finally found the handle to the damned drapes and pulled them across the window. Instincts were screaming at him to get the hell away from there, but some tenacious braggadocio would not permit him to yield to such an uncertain threat. "If you could have pumped me, you'd have pumped me. I don't buy your superman act, and I want to tell you something, guy. When I leave Dallas I'm going to have your head in a sack. Don't think you've made any points with me because of this kind of childish bullshit."

The guy said, "No points intended, Lileo. Just

wanted to show you what I think of your lousy band of head-hunters. Listen to this."

The telephone instrument virtually leapt from Lileo's head as the receiving diaphragm rattled violently with an explosive report and Lileo took a dive.

His ear was ringing and he nearly blacked out for an instant from the auditory shock.

Quaso, too, flung away his telephone and sprawled to the floor, instinctively seeking the lowest horizontal level he could attain.

Another explosive report blasted through the abandoned receivers before the first hard item of confirming evidence could travel the course and a heavy bullet crashed the glass window, ripped through the drapery, and plowed into the paneled wall above the desk like a woodsman's axe, coming in at shoulder level. And they kept coming, one upon another in a coolly calculated pattern that searched that wall right to left then top to bottom directly along the centerline above the desk.

The telephone was lying on the floor beside Lileo's head. He counted ten reports and winced with each impact, and when it was done he heard the cold voice in the receiver, "There you go, head-hunter. Welcome to the war for Texas."

Tough young men were lying all over each other in wall-to-wall cautious flesh, even in those areas far removed from the scene of destruction. Not a man in the place was on his feet.

Lileo lifted his head off the floor and snarled, "The son of a bitch!"

Quaso was staring mutely at his ruined wall. Shards of broken glass littered the area and shredded splinters of wood were still settling.

Someone close by, in a voice that carried throughout the room, cried, "Jesus! Look at that! He put a cross on it. A perfect cross!"

"Through closed fucking drapes," someone added.

And thus grew again the soul-shaking legend of Mack the Bastard—half man, half demigod—the stone-cold killer who had executed more *amici* than all the past Mafia strife in history had accounted for.

Half a mile away, an entirely human being carefully disconnected his lineman's phone from a roof patch, stowed a tripod-mounted rifle in a shoulder bag, and made his withdrawal to a new line in the hell grounds.

And, yes, he had been making points. He had moved caution, respect, and perhaps belly-bunching fear into the hearts of the enemy. It could prove to be an edge that he would sorely need before this night was done.

Sure, he could have taken Lileo and Quaso both, as easy as pie. But to what good effect on the overall objective of this mission?

The game, at this point, was to rattle some teeth —to demoralize the enemy, get them to jumping at every shadow, wincing with every sound of the night.

A confused and overly cautious enemy was likely to make mistakes—crucial ones.

Bolan had not come all this way just for a shoot-out with the head-hunters.

He had come to restore depth to the heart of Texas.

But first he had to put in fear.

And, yes, things were working.

Ten minutes after the fusillade through Jaunty Joe Quaso's penthouse windows, a number of heavily loaded vehicles erupted from the underground garage to form a caravan which sped away toward the inner city.

And, several blocks back, an interested observer in Porsche hot wheels tagged along to scout the next fire line.

14: RUNNING

To give the devil his due, it was a mighty tough job of defense presenting itself to Lileo, Quaso, and company.

It was bad enough that the mob interests were so far-flung and multilayered in Texas; the guy could pop up just about anywhere, and it would take a very fine spread of defenses to cover every eventuality. Add to this the fact that the damned guy had such fantastic mobility and the job became a nightmare.

If you then considered the guy himself and what he could do when he wanted to, then the nightmare became a very real fact of life. The stories about the guy were probably not all that exaggerated, after all. He *was* a stunning son of a bitch. Just look at what he had accomplished in less than twelve hours.

He'd made a raid on the oil field, blitzed the place, made off with a star hostage.

Next he'd popped up in Dallas, coolly invaded the head shed itself and made an idiot of Joe Quaso— knocking off half the palace guard and robbing the safe.

A short while later he turns up at the edge of the state to execute a friend of the friends in El Paso, another in Houston, a third in Austin.

And while the heads were together and trying to

figure a way to cover that type of assault, the cocky bastard makes another audacious hit on the head shed—*while talking to Lileo on the damned telephone!*

It was demoralizing, yeah. It was worse than that. All the boys were walking around on tippytoes, taking every breath like it might be their last and peering into every dark corner like the fiends of hell might come rushing out of there at them.

And that wasn't even the worst part. The guy was shaking hell out of the Texas Plan—that was the worst part. Lileo's force had swarmed into Texas on an offensive mission—the Job: get Bolan. And the bastard had turned the tables before they could even get launched. Now the primary mission was an unnerving job of defense: save Texas from the Bolan crunch.

Yes, the Texas Plan was wobbly already—after only twelve hours of this guy. And the old men in the East were damned unhappy about that. The instructions to Lileo and the Bolan Bunch were quite direct and quite clear: stop that son of a bitch from running wild through Texas!

Stunning, yeah. A stunning son of a bitch.

The problem was to figure some way to turn the tables around again. A show of counterforce, first, to reassure those running-scared friends who were central to the Texas Plan, to get them to stand firm and give Lileo time to set up an offensive of his own. Then to outsmart the smart guy, to set him up and let him walk in and hand over his head.

There had to be a leak somewhere in the organi-

113

zation, that was certain. And the guy was using it to make monkeys of them all.

So . . . why not put the leak to work for the right side?

Lileo told Joe Quaso, as their vehicle wheeled into the new headquarters: "I have a plan, Joe. We're going to get that bastard to running."

"Running where, though?" Quaso muttered worriedly.

"Running wild," Lileo replied. He grinned, looked at his hands, and added, "Yeah. Running hog wild."

Bolan followed the Mafia caravan to an old district close-in to the city, where once undoubtedly the cream of Dallas society lived but which was now a decaying neighborhood in which the fine old mansions of a bygone era had been converted to rooming houses and apartment buildings. Others had been torn out to make room for drive-in restaurants, service stations, and other commercial establishments. Here and there, however, remained a valiant holdout against decay and progress, its splendor slightly tarnished but not entirely eclipsed by the tides of time.

It was one of these latter which proved to be the destination of the Lileo force—a three-story Southern colonial with plantation porches and white columns set on several acres of surrounding grounds, fenced with spiked iron.

The place looked like a hardsite.

Bolan marked the spot for future reference and passed on by.

Those people would keep.

There were more pressing matters to occupy his attention for now.

He stopped at a public phone several blocks along and called a local television station. "Let me speak to the managing editor of your news department," he requested.

"Ringing," the switchboard operator assured him.

A moment later he told another young lady, "This is Mack Bolan. Tell the man, huh."

Following a flustered response and a brief wait, a man's voice came on. "This is Les Moore, newsroom manager. *Who* is this calling?"

Bolan said, "Let's keep this short and quick. What I have to say should verify my identity. The name is Bolan and I am not in Texas for my health but for yours. Swamp rot is festering here in Lone Star country and there's going to be the devil to pay if people here don't come alive and face the problem."

"Uh—Bolan, I've got this on the recorder."

"Be my guest. I want it known that I'm the one who hung the death medals on Spellman, Whitson, and Kilcannon this afternoon. I want it known also that a lot more awards will be handed out during the night."

"Everyone is wondering," the newsman said quickly, "why those particular men—why *them?*"

"Shouldn't be so hard to figure out," Bolan clipped back. "I don't make war on civilians."

"Yeah but—you mentioned others. Are you speaking of people with the stature of the other three? You're going to kill—?"

"My time is limited and I hadn't planned on going into details with you. The only ones who need to worry about the night already know who they are. And I know who they are, that's the important point."

"You want me to put this on the air. Right?"

Bolan said, "Right."

"Okay, but I want something in return."

"Name it."

"A quick interview."

"If it's very quick, okay."

The newsman's voice was crackling with interest. "Why Texas? You're a Mafia-buster. Do we have that much, uh, infiltration here?"

Bolan's voice crackled back, "It's no infiltration, Moore. You're being eaten alive."

"That's hard to believe. There's a border Mafia, sure. But—"

"But hell," Bolan said. "It's like cancer. You don't feel the pain until the terminal stages. The mob is about to eat your whole state. They're into everything, and I mean every vital organ."

"But these men you killed today, Bolan—they were among our most respected citizens. Surely—"

"That's one of your larger problems," Bolan said, quietly interrupting the argument. "Look, it's all the time I have."

"Just one more. Uh, human interest angle. Personal question. Okay?"

"Go," Bolan growled.

"How do you *know?* I mean, when you execute a man like Jerry Whitson, how do you *know?*

Don't you ever have doubts? Don't you ever wake up in a cold sweat and wondering if you *really* know what you're doing?"

"The doubts come before, Moore, not after. If the doubt can't be settled then I don't move. I have to go now."

"Wait, just one—I didn't phrase that right. What I meant to ask is how it feels to be judge and jury over these people. How can you be so sure of your own judgment? To just go out and kill a man without benefit of fair trial. Our whole country is based on the idea of justice and—"

"You said an interview, Moore, not a debate. I háve to go—but I'll tell you this much. If a kid goes out and knocks over a gas station, he knows that he's handing his fate up to our justice system. He could get caught, he could get tried and convicted, he could serve time. That's the system, and it usually works. But we're not talking about that kind of system when we reach the subject of organized crime, big-time crime. These people have nothing but contempt for our quote system unquote. They buy the damned system, they own it, and they use it to their own advantage. They are *above* the system. Okay. I'm outside the system, too. That's where they operate—okay, it's where I operate. When our paths cross, there's a reaction. Don't talk to me about judges and juries in the same breath with *Mafia*."

"They get caught. Our federal prisons are full of big-time crooks who are paying the debt to society."

"Are they? A guy loots the economy of a nation,

murders and tortures and terrorizes according to his own whims, corrupts governments and cannibalizes industries, makes junkies out of your kids, whores out of your women, and pimps out of your elected officials. So he's sitting in Leavenworth on an income tax rap. He's paying a debt?"

"Well . . . at least he's out of circulation."

"No way. These people go out of circulation with a bullet in the head. That's the only way."

The newsman had an idea he could not let go. "But when you simply walk up to a man, put a gun to his head and pull the trigger—isn't that?—I mean, every man deserves his day in court, an opportunity to *face* his accusers."

"They face me every time," Bolan assured his interviewer. "And they know. Believe me, they know."

"Gerald Whitson, too? Did he know? *Why* he was being killed?"

"He knew. These people are their own judge and jury, Moore. I'm just the executioner."

"Yeah," the newsman replied in a choked voice. "Trial by ordeal, eh? If they manage to live, then they're innocent. If you pull the trigger, then they're automatically guilty."

Bolan said, "No, they're automatically dead. I'm going now. If you feel all this strongly about the injustice of my operation, then I'm sure you'll want to get the warning out. Judgment has come to Texas. There is only one way the guilty can evade it. They have to get back into the system."

"What does that mean?"

"It means total surrender. Full disclosure of all illegal acts, confession."

"Oh," the newsman replied, startled by a new understanding. "There *is* an out, then. They can purge themselves."

"The outriders, yeah, the people who are riding along on the Mafia's coattails. Like Whitson, Spellman, Kilcannon. They can rejoin the system and take their chances with legal justice. Or they can take their chances with me. Tonight."

Bolan hung up, returned to the hot wheels, and blended back into the night.

While, in a downtown office building, an excited television news crew was gathering around a tape recorder for a replay of the hottest scoop of the year.

Very soon, now, everybody would be running.

15: FACE OF THE DEVIL

There had been a storm of reaction to what the whole town was referring to as "the Mack Bolan newscast." Several prominent citizens had requested police protection. A US district judge announced his resignation and retirement from the bench. Two members of the Texas legislature quickly followed suit and the governor's office announced that an "in-depth investigation" of the executive branch was "underway."

Police agencies throughout the state girded for a night of fireworks and it was announced that a special federal task force of law enforcement officials had reached Texas soil.

So, yes, the night was unwinding itself in Bolan's wake as his movements sent shock waves from border to border. But the man himself was just getting started.

He made one slow pass around the neighborhood, eyes and instincts alert to ominous signs, then powered into the parking lot beside the building in which Arthur Klingman kept town dwellings.

He was debarking from the Porsche when a guy with New York written all over him stepped from the shadows of the building, flashed an open wallet, and announced, "Building security, sir. I'll have to see your parking permit."

Bolan straightened up and gazed down at the guy. "So look," he invited in a light drawl. "It's on the windshield."

The *mafioso* bent over the low-profile vehicle and never straightened up again. Bolan's knee moved into the small of his back as both arms snaked around the neck into the deadly "Vinh Ha torque." The vertebrae were wrenched loose with a gentle sucking sound and the guy quietly ceased to live.

Bolan helped the body to its natural level and nudged it on beneath the vehicle with his feet.

Even if it had been bright daylight, a casual observer would have wondered what became of the second man—it had happened that quickly and that smoothly.

Bolan went on without a pause, moving swiftly to the rear entrance and stepping into the small lobby there.

He was challenged again immediately by a fat man who came scrambling off the stairway. Bolan sat him right back down with a football kick to the belly and followed through with a stiff-finger jab to the throat. The eyes rolled up and the lids dropped—for a while if not forever. The invader kept right on going, homing to his target and moving on tight numbers.

He hit the fourth-floor landing and swept through into the hallway with the Beretta at attention. A guy lunged away from a door about halfway down, clawing for leather as he whirled into position. The Belle chugged once and the sentry whirled on toward eternity, completing the spin and sprawling face down across the entrance to the Klingman apartment.

Bolan stepped over the body and kicked his way inside.

Two hardmen who had been lounging at the television with beer and sandwiches were falling all over each other as they tried to go from full rest to full survival in a heartbeat. Neither made it. Nine millimeters of zinging death for each punched them back to total rest and deposited them in a twisted litter of spilt sandwiches and overturned beer.

Bolan closed the door and advanced deeper into the apartment. He found Arthur Klingman in a back room, seated quietly at a small desk with a jug of tequila and a neat row of lemon slices.

He was a handsome old man with thick white hair and ruddy face, clear eyes, and a chin that could have led a wagon train across hostile country.

A tough old bird, yeah.

He was dressed in starched khaki, the trouser legs stuffed into Western boots that had seen a lot of use. The hands on that desk had the hard, gnarled look that comes from a lifetime of honest toil.

He stood up, slowly and carefully, alert eyes measuring the dimensions of this stranger behind the gun —big like Texas, tall and straight and ready for anything—and, yeah, Bolan thought, a living symbol of this fantastic state.

"I guess we've come a gusher," Klingman said, and the voice matched the rest of the man.

Bolan tossed a marksman's medal to the desk as he replied, "I guess we have, Klingman."

"Okay. I'm ready."

"I'm not here to pin that medal on you," Bolan said.

Surprise registered in those bright eyes, then curiosity. "Then what do you want?"

"I want to keep a promise to a gutsy lady," Bolan told the pioneer oilman. "I told her I'd do what I could to salvage her daddy."

Klingman's eyes quivered. "You've talked to my girl?"

"I *have* your girl. She's safe and well." Bolan flipped a matchbook to the desk and Klingman immediately snatched it up. "You'll find her there. Room one fifteen. She's waiting for you to come for her. Take some clothes, she doesn't have any. Your buddies kept her drugged and naked, under lock and key."

The angry sweep of a forearm sent the tequila hurtling off the desk. "Sonsabitches!" Klingman exploded. Raging eyes found their level in the cool Bolan gaze, then dropped off. "Guess I'm the biggest one of all," he added, the voice deflated.

"That's for you to sift out for yourself," Bolan told him.

"How much do you know?"

"Most of it. Judith helped. I'm up on Flag Seven. The Texas Plan. And I'm going to bust it. With or without your help."

"You want *my* help?"

Bolan gave the old man a curt nod. "Judith feels that you would welcome the option."

Klingman stepped away from the desk.

Bolan put the Beretta away.

The big oilman stood in the center of the room, swaying like a tall Texas pine in a stiff breeze, eyes raised to the ceiling.

He grabbed the back of his neck in a big paw and said, "I *started* Flag Seven, you know."

Bolan said, "I know. Now's your chance to bury it. It's gotten away from you, Klingman. Face that."

"I've tried to," the Texan replied, sighing. "Over and over I've tried to face it. But—damn it!—there has to be a way through!"

"No way through," Bolan assured him. "You bargained with the devil, Klingman. I can almost admire you for that. You placed it all on the line, and I can understand that kind of commitment. But there are no bargains from hell. And now you have to face that truth."

"I don't have to face anything!" the oilman roared.

"You have to face your daughter," Bolan quietly reminded him. "Or you have to face me. That's your option."

The Texan grinned, and Bolan saw in there the origins of Judith Klingman's gutsy humor. "I'd rather face the devil than either of you," the old man said. "I caught your television show. Very convincing. And the coyotes are howling all over Texas. Bolan, you can believe this or not. I have had no controlling hand in Flag Seven since the coyotes started prowling our flanks. You're right. It got away from me. A bargain with the sonsabitchin' devil—you're right there, too. But it started as a pure idea—or almost, anyway."

Bolan glanced at his watch. "My time has run out here," he said. "We can talk while we travel. Let's go."

"Where to?"

"To face the devil, maybe."

Klingman said, "Just a minute." He dragged a briefcase from a book shelf and told the Executioner, "This will save a lot of talk. And it's the devil's truth, every word of it. Maps, plans, timetables, the whole thing. Take it and git. I'll just slow you down, and I can get Judith on my own."

"We leave together," Bolan replied firmly. He took the pioneer Texan's arm and steered him toward the door.

"And we'll probably end up in hell together," Klingman muttered.

Bolan already knew that.

He'd faced the devil, himself, many times.

But never over the body of a defeated old man. Understandable pressures had turned Arthur Klingman—and some of the men with him—onto this detour to damnation. At least they had been men enough to place their souls on the line for an honest commitment. So it had turned sour—from too much seasoning in the pot. More than a dash of greed, a sprinkling of lunacy, and finally the big Mafia hambone.

Despite the claims of his detractors, Mack Bolan did not play God. He neither judged nor condemned men like Klingman. Each man, he knew, was his own judge and his own condemnation.

And maybe Klingman was right. Maybe the two

of them would walk the bitter shores of hell together.

But not tonight, hopefully. He dropped the old man at a safe point and went on to gather the next numbers of the night.

With the face of the devil hovering all over that land.

16: THE KICKER

Jack Grimaldi's voice came across the line tense and nervous. "Man I'm glad you checked in. Something's wrong out at that motel. The chick has either flown or can't answer the phone. I've been ringing every five minutes since I got here."

Bolan's response was slow in coming. "Well," he replied presently, "she's a free agent."

"Maybe she's just afraid to answer the phone. I thought of that, too."

"No. I told her to expect a call. Damn. I just sent Arthur Klingman out there. Well . . . he's a pretty capable old bird. I'll let him worry it from there. The other numbers are falling. Get the chopper ready."

"She's ready. When and where do you want her?"

"Not sure yet. I'm just laying back now and reading the opposition. But I want to be ready to spring with them. Stick close to that phone."

"Will do. Uh, I have a piece of intelligence for you."

"I told you to stay low, Jack."

"I'm low. But, hell, can't just sit here and crack my knuckles all night. I was calling around, trying to pick up something—maybe some whispers about the Klingman chick. Nothing there, not a peep in the hen house, but I got something else may interest you."

"Okay, unload it."

"Lileo has sent a hard force out to that joint we hit this morning, Klingman's Wells. It seems that we missed something out there, something big. The story I get, there's about a square mile of camouflage netting strung up just west of there—and some mighty interesting things are supposed to be beneath that netting."

"What sort of things?"

"Crazy things. If the intel is straight, it's a staging area for a paramilitary force."

"Okay, I'll buy that," Bolan said. Sure, a sprinkling of insanity.

"And more than that. They're stockpiling crude oil out there in concealed tanks. I hear they've also got a secret pipeline coming in from some refinery and they're storing gasoline and jet aviation fuel. This guy tells me they've got row upon row of military armored cars under that netting. Also ammunition dumps and the whole military picture. No troops, though. They've got them dispersed and out of sight in the civil population. Now they're wanting to disperse the staging depot, too. So Lileo and Quaso have rushed this hard force out there to protect the operation."

"Who'd you get this from, Jack?"

"A guy close to the headshed, a crew boss with Quaso. Pushes Superchicks around Dallas and Fort Worth. You suspect it?"

"I suspect everything," Bolan replied tiredly.

"Well—if it's a plant then they've added a certain

kicker. As the story goes, they're blowing up Klingman's Wells at dawn."

"For what reason?"

"To cover what they've been doing with those wells, I guess. I hear there's still enough crude down there to run the country's vehicles for a year. But they say they're going to blow them. Could they do that?"

According to the intel from Klingman's briefcase, they sure could. Bolan told his pilot, "Yeah, they could lift the whole lease clear off the face of Texas."

"Well, that's the kicker."

"Some kicker," Bolan commented unhappily.

"Well, who gives a shit if they blow up a few wells, eh? You think they're trying to draw you out there with a threat like that? Who gives a shit?"

"There's the problem, Jack. In a few months, I hear, the whole world will be giving one."

"What's that mean?"

"It means we're supposed to be moving steadily toward an energy crisis. Worldwide."

"Oh, that. Well, you know, you hear stories everywhere."

"Only this one is chillingly true, I'm afraid," Bolan replied in a wearied voice. "It's what this whole nutty Texas Plan is about."

"What is that Texas Plan?"

"Another chilling story. A preview, maybe, of what's going to be happening all over the world in a few more years. Territorial wars, Jack. No more fighting over political ideals, but fighting for survival in a world fast running out of natural resources."

"Hell you lost me somewhere between Texas and the world."

"I'll fill you in later. But we have to go back to Klingman's, Jack. So get that bird hot and ready."

"What the hell has this got to do with the mob?"

"They're the ants, Jack."

"The what?"

"At every picnic there's a swarm of ants. Right? And the biggest picnic in the country right now is Texas oil."

"Hey! I'm beginning to get the—"

"Right, it's a lot bigger than we thought. Stay ready, Jack. I'll be calling."

Bolan hung up and returned to his vehicle, survival instincts as alert as ever but the intellectual side of his mind in the depths of thought.

Sure. It could be the last picnic in Texas. And after that—where?

Wherever oil was king, probably.

And at the moment—or at a very early future moment, at least—whoever controlled the oil of the world would indeed control the whole world.

Yes, it was a chilling thought.

No wars had been seen that would match the desperate ferocity of affluent nations battling for their share of industrial survival.

And, yes, Mack Bolan "gave a shit" about the fate of a few wells in Texas.

He would, if necessary, give his final heartbeat. While he lived, the mob was not going to muscle into the big picnic in Texas.

Grimaldi's "intelligence" had a smell to it, sure.

Inside information such as that does not simply drop from the skies, not unless somebody is pushing it with a purpose.

Would those dum-dums actually blow up those wells? Even if Bolan did not accept the bait? Or even if he did?

Bolan had to shake his head over that one. He did know that the capability was there—the intel from Klingman himself verified that much. The entire Klingman Petro lease was wired for destruction.

Yeah. The Executioner would have to go check that out—bait for hell or not.

First, though, he had a couple of dates to keep. One with a man from Washington.

And another with a crafty dude from St. Looey.

The Executioner had a "kicker" of his own in mind.

17: A SEVENTH FLAG FOR TEXAS

Bolan halted at the main entrance to the Federal Building and flashed his lights.

Harold Brognola moved casually to the sidewalk, opened the door, and slid in beside the most wanted man in America.

"Some wheels," was his greeting.

The Porsche moved smoothly from the curb and into the stream of evening traffic. The Executioner told the chief of the federal get-Bolan task force, "Mob money bought it. Tell them."

Brognola grunted and lit a cigarette. He was a man of fortyish years, medium height and weight, with a deceptively amiable appearance. He might have been a shoe salesman, harriedly preparing for a Christmas shopping rush but grimly determined to maintain the holiday cheer. He was, in fact, a federal agent with a law degree and many years of frustration in his chosen field—racket-busting. During the early days of the Bolan wars, Brognola had managed to make personal contact with the most effective racket-buster of them all and had subsequently launched a quiet campaign to give Bolan hush-hush support by the federal government—but Bolan himself had declined the arrangement.

The one-man army had once told Brognola: "The tracks I make with my own blood are my tracks alone and my responsibility alone. I don't like the idea of dragging the whole country into hell with me."

It was this side of the Executioner that commanded such respect from this man who had dedicated his life to "justice under the law." Even after Brognola had been officially accorded prime responsibility in the government's campaign to apprehend Mack Bolan, that respect had remained intact and had in fact created a troubling conflict of interests.

"The guy is no mad dog killer," Brognola had once told his chief. "We can trust him to pick and choose the proper targets. He is the best weapon to come along in the battle against organized crime. The man deserves a portfolio."

But "the man" would not accept that portfolio. And the governmental pressures on Brognola had become intense.

At one particularly low point in their relationship, in Vegas, Brognola had personally gone a'gunning for the Executioner, however regretfully. It had been a "mad dog hunt" at Vegas—both Brognola and Bolan had understood that clearly. Mack Bolan would not fire upon the law, Brognola knew that also. Only providence had averted a tragic ending to that Vegas encounter. Thereafter, Brognola had walked a delicate line between his sense of duty and his sense of respect and admiration for this committed hellfire guy.

And now here they were, together again in a tense situation, friendly opponents and often grudging allies, with governmental pressures at an all-time peak of get-Bolan fever.

Brognola worked at the cigarette through several nervous inhalations; then he told the big cool man beside him, "I want you to bow out of Texas. That's a personal request, and you can look at it any way you choose. Call it a collection on the debt of past favors. Call it love, fear, or just plain chickenshit. But I want you out of this state by midnight."

The Porsche was cruising, flowing with the traffic. Bolan said, "I don't expect to be finished by midnight, Hal."

"You're finished right now," the fed replied amiably. "You've done enough. The rats are fleeing the ship right now. Let us take it from here. You split. We'll pick up the rest of the marbles."

"You don't even know where the marbles are," Bolan said in a flattened voice.

"We may know more than you think."

Bolan growled, "You're onto Flag Seven, then."

"Flag what?"

"So you're not," Bolan concluded.

"Now hold it."

Bolan chuckled. It was the sound of icicles shattering on frozen ground. "You want to move that deadline?" he asked.

Brognola fidgeted and smoked. Presently he replied, "How much time do you need?"

"It started at dawn," Bolan said. "I expect to finish it by then."

The official head jerked in quick agreement. "Okay. I'll give my marshals a night's sleep. But that's as far as I can stretch. You've stepped on some big toes down here, friend. At dawn, my marshals go a'gunning. Call that fair warning . . . from a friend. Now what is this flag business?"

"They call it Flag Seven," Bolan explained. "Brain child of one Arthur Klingman, a big—"

"I know the name," Brognola reported, sighing.

"So does every hood in the country, now," Bolan said. "The thing ran away from the old man. It started as a simple reaction to a big squeeze from some of the giant oil companies. Klingman saw the handwriting on the wall, figured the days of the independent oilmen were numbered. These native Texans are tough people, Hal. Especially those who grew up in a wildcatter's bunkhouse. Well, they organized into this secret operation which they called Flag Seven. A symbol of their independent spirit, I guess. But that's all it was at first—a symbol. And maybe a statement of determination to keep *Texas* independent from the big international manipulators. I could sympathize with that. But then the nuts began crawling out of Arthur Klingman's woodwork, and they flat took him over. A lunatic political fringe and a powerful economic power bloc combined to make Flag Seven the master plan for the new Texas Republic, and I mean for real. They even have a small paramilitary force and a handle on this state you wouldn't believe."

"That explains Spellman, then," Brognola commented with obvious interest.

"It does. Nat Spellman was their intelligence honcho. He has the whole damned state wired for sound,

135

even the governor's mansion. Besides that, the guy engineered a really fantastic snoop-drop from the big national communications relay at El Paso."

Brognola looked appalled. "That's crazy! What are they shooting for?—another civil war?"

Bolan shrugged. "I don't know. This is the looney part. I thought at first that they were just going for a political and economic takeover. But, hell . . . I have evidence now that there's a lot more involved than that. These guys are serious about this Seventh Flag over Texas. They're going for the big one—a revival of the Republic of Texas, no less."

"It's crazy," Brognola said uneasily.

"Crazy, but dangerous as hell," Bolan assured him. "It's the coalition of interests that just could make it work. They already had the strong political core and a fearsome economic base. And now that the boys have joined the picnic . . . well, this state is up for grabs, Hal."

"It's still crazy. I don't see how they could hope to . . ."

Bolan's voice was tinged with incredulity itself as he moved deeper into the explanation. "I know. It sounds nutty. Especially for the mob. Those guys always have their feet squarely on the ground. But . . . most people probably don't realize how important Texas is to this country. Oil alone, hell. Do you know how much of our petroleum comes from this state? About a third."

"Yeah. Hold it a minute, will you. Give me a chance to think into this." Brognola crushed out his cigarette and immediately lit another.

Bolan drove on in silence, picking his way through the traffic and apparently doing some "thinking in" of his own.

After a moment, Brognola exhaled a hissing column of cigarette smoke and said, "Yeah. A lot of little things . . . they're falling in now. You're right about Texas, of course. It's the richest political subdivision in the world. Not just for its oil, either. Hell it's big in everything—in mineral production, chemicals, agriculture, manufactured goods—hell, yes. I don't find it too surprising that some large brains would like to carve it out of the 'subdivision' status and raise their own flag over it. But I don't see how they could pull it off. It's just too big, too ambitious to—"

Bolan said tightly, "Speaking of big, did you know that it is farther from El Paso to Beaumont than from New York to Chicago? That's part of the problem, Hal. I've noticed that the police agencies down here have a hell of a problem that way, too. How the hell do you police a state that's bigger than the whole Northeastern section of the country? They couldn't cover it all with flying patrols, even."

"Okay. But forget about cops. You can't just pull a state out of this union. Abe Lincoln proved that. Are these guys ready for a war with the United States of America?"

"Maybe so," Bolan mused. "There's more than one way to war. I know this much. These guys mean business."

Brognola shook his head. "I still don't see a *modus*."

"Blackmail," Bolan said.

"What?"

"They grab political control, by clout and by stacking both political parties with their own men. Then they lay all over everything and seize the economy. Forget federal courts and federal resources. There will be no federal resources on Texas soil—it will be *Texas* resources. Texas wealth for Texans, that will be the gig. Let Wall Street and Zurich and every other financial capital in the world throw tantrums—these guys intend to sit down here beneath their seventh flag and thumb their noses at the whole damned world."

"It doesn't hold together," Brognola argued. "It's like a scenario for a science fiction movie."

"That's what it is," Bolan agreed. "Except that they have the perfect kicker."

"What kicker?"

"Oil."

"Huh?"

"Oil."

There was another long silence. Then Brognola said, "Well I'll be damned."

Bolan said, "Yeah."

"They, in effect, nationalize the oil industry of Texas—only now it's the Republic of Texas. Anybody who wants to buy Texas oil had better be damned nice about it."

Bolan said, "Yeah. It could work. Handled just right, it could work. And look at the talent they have now. *Cosa di tutti Cosi.* This is it, Hal. The grand slammer."

"Let me skull this some more."

"Skull it on your own time. I have work to do."

"Baloney. We *both* have work to do. And don't give me any of that independent agent bullshit, either. Drive around some more."

Bolan grinned solemnly and made another cut across town.

Brognola said, "Petroleum clout, that's what it boils down to. The hell of it, Mack, is that there really is an energy problem facing this country. I was talking to a member of the President's energy council just the other day. The guy was damned worried. We could be into gas rationing before long. The big worry on this guy's mind was Mafia exploitation of the problem—hijacks, black market rings, that sort of thing. But hell! Who would have thought that the boys would try to corner the whole damned market!"

"Just how real is this energy problem, Hal?"

"Very real. We're running out."

"How about imports?"

"Yeah, how about that," Brognola grumped. "We don't have enough deep-water ports for the supertankers. We don't have enough refinery capacity. We don't have enough—"

"Okay, it's real," Bolan said. "So, with a cut-off of Texas oil, the country is in deep trouble. For real."

"For very real."

"Then it's going to be a gut-buster," Bolan decided. "Stop wondering if these guys can pull off the Texas heist. The try itself will be enough to send the whole thing a'toppling."

"I don't—"

"Be quiet and listen. I told you they have themselves a junior army. Well that's for real, too. Each man is trained in demolitions. I mentioned blackmail. Here's how they will try. Paramilitary teams will swarm the oil fields and occupy them. They will shut down the refineries and stop the pumps on the wells and pipelines. They've been practicing on Klingman property, learning the tricks. Meanwhile there will have been a hard sell to the people from the propaganda mills, selling Texas to Texans—and that's not hard to sell in these parts. They—"

"Hold it," Brognola snapped. "Back up to that occupation of the oil fields. Is that their battle line?"

"It is. They've been working quietly for months, setting the thing up. They are dooms-daying the oil-fields."

"They are what?"

"You heard it. It's a go-for-broke operation. They're rigging wells all over the state for self-destruct, and that's where the blackmail enters the picture. Sure, Uncle Sam is a pretty big guy to tackle. But even that dude is going to back off and think twice before he risks the loss of a third of his oil reserves. And they know what they're doing, these boys. The Klingman lease has been set up as the proof site. It's wired for doomsday right now. Meanwhile they're pumping like mad and getting all the oil out they can, storing it somewhere out there in concealed storage depots. I don't believe they really want to blow that field, but they will if they get pushed."

"It's insane," Brognola muttered.

"Sure it is. But so was Hitler, and look at all the hell that guy brought to earth. It's a gut-buster, Hal, any way you slice it. And I'm not bowing out—not at midnight and not at dawn, either, unless I take all the crazy men out with me."

"It could spread," the federal man observed gloomily. "Stuff like this is contagious. What if Louisiana and Oklahoma decided to shut down, too. What if all the oil and gas states decide to declare a petroleum republic."

Bolan said, "It would be a natural reaction."

"Sure it would. And not just in this country. South America could get snotty. Canada already has. The Arabs could all go crazy. Hell! You ever get the feeling that our civilization is a very fragile thing?"

Bolan replied, "I live with the feeling."

"I guess you do," the man from Washington quietly agreed. He crushed his cigarette into the ashtray and clasped his hands behind his head. "So tell me something to make me feel better."

"I've rattled some teeth. The saner ones are already bailing out, like you said. Klingman himself bailed out a long time ago, in his heart anyway. The mob was holding his daughter to keep him in line. I've taken out their intelligence chief, the propaganda minister, and the top money man. Right behind you, you will find a briefcase. Take it with you. It probably won't convince anybody in Washington that this problem is for real, but it could help."

"Okay, thanks. How's your hide?"

Bolan grinned. "Still intact. I've got the boys down here walking cautious. I hope to keep them that way."

"Who's on board?"

"The local punk is Joe Quaso. Guy named Lileo arrived today with about a hundred guns. Quaso's force is spread too thin to cause me much trouble. Lileo is another story. I'll have to rattle his cage again, and very soon."

"Don't, uh, give these Texas cops too much daylight. They're tough."

Bolan nodded. "Thanks. I'm keeping my distance."

"And watch that Lileo guy. I just got him into my files. He's a rotten little Mississippi mud stomper with head-busting ambitions. A very, very dangerous man."

"What's his credentials?"

"The terror of Bourbon Street. Enforced the Biloxi area for a couple of years. Started as an arm breaker, graduated to the big time via a couple of land speculation deals in which several principals mysteriously disappeared and turned up later in a Louisiana swamp. The guy has Cajun blood, via his mother, and Mafia blood from about six generations. His old man was a personal consort of Huey Long and he has an uncle presently very large in Louisiana politics."

"Pedigree?"

"Arrested about a dozen times, Louisiana and Mississippi. No convictions."

Bolan sighed. "Okay. He's due for a rattle."

"Drop me."

"Sure." Bolan hit the wheel and made a beeline toward the pickup point. "How many guns do you have for the party tonight?"

"Enough. Tell me where you definitely will not be."

Bolan smiled as he replied, "I definitely will not be in the vicinity of Klingman's Wells."

"Okay. I'll cover the other possibilities. Uh, what's happening at Klingman's?"

"I was invited."

"I see. They're not, uh, thinking of blowing that fucking place up tonight, I hope."

Bolan replied, "Thinking is not doing."

"Whatever that means, eh?"

Bolan grinned. "It means they're not, by God, going to."

Brognola sighed heavily and pulled Arthur Klingman's briefcase into his lap.

Bolan pulled to the curb.

Brognola opened the door, then paused and turned a tight smile to the damnedest guy he'd ever known, "Tallyho, soldier. Good hunting. Burn a flag for me, eh?"

Then he was out and the door slammed shut, and Bolan was alone again with the night.

Brognola, he knew, would be burning a few flags for himself in this would-be new republic before the night was done.

Yeah. It was going to be a damned busy night for Texas. And Bolan knew the name of his game now.

It was called, "Save Texas for the sane Texans."

That was it. Melodramatic though it may sound, that was the all of it.

And it was time for the games to begin.

18: HAYMAKER

It was just past nine o'clock when the Porsche hot-wheeled up to the gate of the old mansion in Dallas.

The gateman stepped to the window to peer in at the occupant of the vehicle. Bolan showed the guy a scowl and said, *"Amici."* It meant *friend*, even on Texas soil, but the sentry appeared to have some doubts about that.

Before the *mafioso* could get his mind set, though, Bolan flooded it with a stream of words. "Christ, I been all over this town looking for you boys. First of all the fucking goddamn airport is fifty miles across the horizon and I never seen such a flat-ass country in my life before. I was afraid I might fall off the other fucking edge if I ever got there. Forget Columbus, hey, and the fucking goddamn Atlantic ocean. Lookit Texas, man, lookit all that flat nothing spread out there. And this goddamn *town*, man. It stretches to everywhere, and still there's nothing there. And that's where I been the past two hours, man, *no* fucking where! What the hell are we doing in this crummy neighborhood?"

The guy was showing him a broad, understanding grin. "Hey," he said amiably, "wait'll you see these fucking goddamn Texas *women*, though. Ain't nothing flat about *them*. Where you down from?"

"Jersey," Bolan shot back. "I'm supposed to check

145

in with Mr. Lileo pers'nally. And please, hey, don't tell me he ain't here."

The gateman laughed and said, "He's here, relax." He jerked a thumb and added, "Go on up to the house. Go easy, though. The boss's on the balls of his feet tonight."

Bolan allowed his gaze to stray about the grounds. They were dark, forbidding—but without obvious patrols. He craned his head through the window to ask in a conspiratorial tone, "That why we're mobbed up in this old joint? Things get hot already?"

"Hot you ain't dreamed of yet," the gateman assured the Executioner. "So don't go blowing in with a lot of chatter if you know what's good for you. You know, eh?"

Bolan knew, precisely. He eased on along the drive and parked on the lawn across from the house.

A couple of boys stepped to the porch railing to ogle the car. He gave a cheery wave as he came out of there and called over, "Relax, boys, the great white hope from Jersey has arrived. Now you can all go to bed."

One of the men waved back and sent a quiet jeering sound with it.

Bolan walked around to the rear of the Porsche and opened the storage compartment. Snugly secured in there lay a favored weapon, the M-16/M-79 over-'n'-under configuration. The 16 would spit a steady trail of 7.62mm tumblers at almost the speed of lightning. The mighty 79 was a heavy firepower piece, breechloading 40mm rounds of high-explosive, fragmentation, double-aught buck, smoke or gas—depending upon the druthers of the situation.

He slung a ready-belt across his shoulders and hoisted the weapon to his chest, then walked across the drive and onto the lawn directly in front of the house.

He was nonchalantly feeding a round of HE into the M-79 breech when one of the men on the porch called over, "What the *hell* is that?"

"It's doomsday," the Executioner called back. His finger grazed the M-16 trigger and a figure eight pattern of hi-velocity tumblers swept the two men away from the railing and deposited them in a heap at the wall.

In a continuation of the same fluid motion, Bolan angled the weapon a few degrees left and let go the M-79 round. It hit the door dead center with flaming thunder and disintegrated it.

The sound of that thunderous blast was echoing from the white columns along the porch when a hardman came pounding around the corner of the house on a dead run, making the scene just in time to catch another stream of tumblers across the chest.

A round of double-aughts clicked into the breech of the 79 and immediately sped away toward that smoking doorway, instantly cooling that area of any hot interest which could be developing there.

A hand and a pistol appeared at a lighted upstairs window. A round of HE flew that way, impacting just below the window sill. That entire section of wall fell away, screaming man and window and all crashing to the flowerbeds below.

Hasty feet were pounding the turf somewhere out in the darkness. Bolan thumbed in a round of tear gas and fired for the ground in that sector, then followed with a searching pattern from the M-16.

He was pacing about in front of the house, right at the fringe of darkness, coolly selecting targets and sending hot war a'winging wherever his attention centered—and the entire joint was in total pandemonium, unseen men stampeding and yelling, flames shooting everywhere—and very quickly there was no darkness anywhere about those grounds.

Sporadic and totally ineffective return fire was beginning to come in from several quarters of those grounds, but none from the house itself. Those people in there were scrambling just to keep their bodies intact.

Bolan sent a few more rounds of HE inside and followed with a shot of gas to each floor, then he returned to the Porsche, stowed the weapon, and got out of there.

He'd planned no more than a wild haymaker, after all. A hit and run, and it was time to run.

For someone else, too. The gateman had just come unglued from his station and was panting up the drive. Bolan screeched to a halt, took a pistol from the guy's hand without protest, and replaced it with a marksman's medal.

"Give that to Lileo," he instructed. "Whether he's dead or alive."

The guy just gawked at him, and he was still rooted to his tracks when the Porsche screamed on through the gate and back into no man's land.

"There you go, *amici*," Bolan muttered into the rearview mirror.

148

There was no way of knowing how much actual damage had been done—and Bolan did not particularly care. The joint was gone, sure. Already the flames were leaping high above the treetops and lighting the neighborhood.

The actual damage could not be measured in property or blood, though. These boys had come to Texas for a war, and they were learning just how hot an Executioner war could get.

There was the value.

"And now," Bolan said, speaking only to the hot wheels, "we trade you in for a set of rotary wings."

This war was due to become much hotter, very quickly.

And Bolan was perhaps a bit modest in the assessment of that latest haymaker to the mob's Texas headshed.

At that moment a tattered and bleeding chief honcho was staggering from the shattered mansion and finding a place of rest upon the grass outside. Two of his men followed quickly behind, bearing the blackened remains of once-jaunty Joe Quaso. They dumped the body unceremoniously onto the ground beside the boss and went back for more. Lileo took a sickened look and hastily averted his eyes from the mess.

All the Superchicks in Dallas could not put that guy together again.

And the boss of the Bolan Bunch was already gripped by the cold reality of the moment when the gate guard knelt beside him and held out the little medal. "He said you should get this, boss," the hardman reported.

Lileo batted the hand away and spat after it. "How'd he get *in* here?" he asked in a coldly controlled voice.

"I dunno, boss," the man lied. "All of a sudden here he was just. Blazing away at everybody. I never saw nothing like that before."

"You're never going to see it again, either," Lileo promised. "Get the cars around here and let's split before the badges arrive."

"Where we going, boss?"

"We're going after that guy, that's where. I want that guy so bad I can taste his blood on my tongue."

"Me too, boss."

Lileo knew better.

The shaking sonuvabitching two-bit gunsel wanted nothing so much as getting the hell out of this state. Probably most of the boys felt that way, those that were left living and able to move.

"Bring those cars around!" Lileo snarled. "I'm doubling the bonuses on this trip. Spread that around. Did you see the guy's car? Did you see it?"

"Yessir, I saw it, a new Porsche, gray, and I'd say superhot."

"Form a caravan! Don't leave no bodies laying around, load them all in. Let's go! Let's go!"

The big chase was on.

Clear to hell.

19: MISSION CONTROL

It was nearing eleven o'clock. The base camp Holiday Inn was having a pretty good night of it. "Steve & Willie" were entertaining in the lounge and enjoying a pretty good draw. The parking area was filled at that end of the place but spotted with empty spaces on the back lot for lodgers.

Grimaldi spoke through the intercom to verify Bolan's intentions. "You sure you want to set down there? These birds draw a lot of attention wherever they land."

"Put her down on the back lot," Bolan instructed. "As close to the war wagon as you can get. You make the hardware transfer. Bring aboard as much as we can carry. Concentrate on the heavy stuff."

Grimaldi nodded in understanding and made a quick drop to treetop level, then maneuvered cautiously into an open area about twenty feet from the van. They settled in with a gentle bump and the pilot quickly cut the power.

Bolan opened the hatch, tapped his watch with a finger, and repeated another important order. "If I'm not back in two minutes, get going and don't look back."

He was rigged for combat, in black suit and full supporting regalia. The AutoMag rode the right hip in military leather. The Beretta was snugged-in

151

beneath the left arm. Utility belts hugged the chest in crossing diagonals to support ammo clips and dangling munitions of varying capabilities.

He was moving on tight numbers and he had a job of scouting which could not wait for a tomorrow that may never come.

He hit the door at room 115, looked in, closed it up and went on without pause, across the pool-patio enclosure where several late hangers-on watched his transit with unblinking curiosity, and into the lobby at full stride.

Several couples were standing about in there, apparently awaiting seating in the lounge. Through the open doorway the amplified rock sounds of Steve & Willie were competing in an even match with the buzz of voices raised in carefree community.

A tired looking man in travel-rumpled slacks and stained shirt gave awed way to his place at the registry desk, stepping back to give the armed warrior an "I-don't-believe-it-but-I-guess-anything-can-happen-in-Texas" inspection and plenty of elbow room.

The clerk looked as though he did not wish to believe it, either, but this was no reason to lose his official cool. "Yes sir, can I help you, sir?" he asked smoothly.

Bolan dropped a medal on the desk.

The clerk looked at it, picked it up, said, "Yes, Mr. Bolan, yes, sir."

"There was a lady in one fifteen," Bolan stated flatly. "Don't screw me around, I'm in a hurry. What happened to the lady?"

The guy's eyes were longingly searching the lobby for some evidence of imminent assistance. But the place had cleared, magically, and the sudden silence from the lounge indicated only that he was being watched with interest from afar.

He hung a smile in front of that icy Bolan gaze and told the most talked-about man in Texas: "A blonde lady, yes sir, it's interesting you should ask about her. Another man—an older gentlemen—was here just a short while ago on the same—"

Bolan snapped, "Ten seconds, mister. Where is she?"

"I'm trying to tell you. I haven't seen the lady in one fifteen. But the day man—he recognized her from the photo—he told them he saw her during a police inspection this morning—I don't—"

"Told who?"

"The two men who came in this evening. We were changing shifts. Grover was still here. That's the day man, Grover Sills. These men had a photo of a beautiful blonde. The one man said she was his wife and he was looking for her. The other man tried to slip each of us a twenty—said he was a private detective. Grover recognized the lady and—"

Bolan growled, "Describe the men."

The guy gave a hopeless shrug. The pupils of his eyes were showing the strain of the interrogation—they seemed to be growing. Official cool was departing rapidly. This was a situation plainly not covered at motel training school. A hubbub of reaction was beginning to swell from the lounge. Two elderly ladies were standing on the patio just outside, faces pressed curiously to the glass wall, staring in with hands cupping their eyes.

Bolan's hands were pressed stiffly upon the desk top, the knuckles showing white. He said, "I'm not going to hurt you. It's life or death for that girl. Damn it, give me something."

The clerk came unfroze. He said, "The man who claimed to be her husband was very . . . mean looking. A real tough guy, you know. And he talked . . . funny."

"Funny how?"

"Well like . . . like . . ."

Bolan helped. "Like an animal."

"Yes sir. He sort of growled and snorted as he spoke."

Bolan said, "Thanks. For the lady, too." He spun around and went out of there, moving quickly on dwindling numbers.

The blades of the copter were turning in a slow idle and a number of curious folk had formed an observation line along the side of the building when Bolan rejoined.

Grimaldi showed him a strained smile as he reported, "I got most of it. How'd you do?"

"Lift off," Bolan commanded and closed the hatch.

The engine revved and the little bird lurched upward.

Bolan got into his headset and reported his find to the man beside him. "Woofer snatched her back."

The pilot's eyes marveled at that. "How the hell did he find her?"

"Simple, methodical police work. Sometimes I have to wonder who are the better cops."

"I warned you about that guy. He's got instincts."

"Yeah. Klingman was here asking questions, too. I imagine he got the same info I got."

Grimaldi asked, "Does this change the plan?"

"It does not. It looks like all trails lead to the same target."

"To the wells, then."

"That is affirmative," Bolan replied grimly.

Sure. The numbers were all falling in. And another campaign was reaching critical mass—the final flash-point.

Bolan became aware of that familiar coldness centering in his chest. No two campaigns were ever entirely alike. Each had its own targets, its own hazards, its own unique problems. And each one had seemed uniquely urgent.

But they all shared a common denominator. The responsibility for it all lay squarely upon the shoulders of this lone individual. This did not downgrade the value of a guy like Grimaldi. But in the final equation, guys like Grimaldi simply made the campaign larger by their very presence. They increased the personal responsibility of Bolan simply because they widened the scope of the job at hand.

And that coldness in Bolan's chest was fear, sure. But it was not a fear of dying or of suffering. He had known forever that there was but one way out of this lousy war for the Executioner. He would war until he died, and he had long ago accepted the inevitable fact that he would die warring and damned.

That was not the fear which this living dead man carried into each flashpoint.

The fear was of failure.

Could he pull it off? With so much riding on his every move and simplest decision, could he thread that eye of storm and pull everything through the other side?

Damn it, he *had* to pull it off. Too much was at stake even to contemplate failure.

"Affirmative," he repeated to Jack Grimaldi. "The target is confirmed. The mission is go."

Yeah. Come hell and damnation or whatever else the night may hold, the numbers were all coming together at Klingman's Wells—where they had started.

The eye of the storm had closed in upon itself.

20: DROP ZONE

It was midnight, and the Woofer was insuring that the guard was changing in a military manner. There would be no more by God goof-ups like that terrible mishap of the morning.

He was walking with a limp, thanks to that bastard in black and his fancy fireworks, but he would walk on his goddamn hands to get another crack at that guy.

He could have left a small force at that motel, sure, just in case the guy did come back there. But the Klingman chick had enough sense slapped into her that he believed her story. The guy had not planned to return to that motel.

Woofer trusted his instincts, though. He knew that Bolan would find out about the girl. And it seemed a dead certainty that the guy would come gunning back for her.

And this is where Woofer wished to meet the Executioner—on his own sod again, but this time under his own carefully planned conditions.

The runway was mined. Let him try landing there again.

The fence was electrified, with high voltage. Let the fancy bastard put one paw on it.

All the tricky security gimmicks laid in here by the general—electronic systems that Tolucci had once sneered at—let the smartass find a way inside the compound—and *bang!*—they'd have the guy in a steel trap that a goddamn infantry company couldn't fight their way out of.

First, Quaso had reinforced him. Then Lileo sent over a force. Coupled with Tolucci's Mexicans, he had a God damn impregnable armed camp here.

So, sure, let fancypants Bolan try Tolucci once more. He'd show the bastard that Jim the Animal didn't get that nickname just by the way he talked.

The Mexican corporal was showing his *El Capitain* a dazzling smile and assuring him that the guard force was posted and alert.

Tolucci pulled his mind out of its grim thoughts and he told the corporal, "I catch a man asleep and I'll shoot him where he lays. They better all understand that."

"*Si, Capitain.* The *soldados* will not fail you again."

Tolucci nodded and moved off toward the house, then halted in quivering alertness and raised his eyes to the black sky. "Did you hear that?" he asked the corporal.

The guy said nothing, but his face was tilted skyward also.

Then Tolucci heard the distant sound again.

"A chopper!" he snarled, and snatched a solid-state radio from his belt to alert the force. "Eyes and ears open!" he commanded via the radio. "Something's coming in. Watch it down! And goddamn it I want a ring of steel where it lands!"

He pushed a special button on the radio and floodlight sprang into brilliance throughout the compound; then he hurried toward the *hacienda* to man the command post.

The unmistakable egg-beater sounds of the helicopter continued growing louder and accompanied the head cock across the grounds. Navigation lights became visible, then a landing flood.

The chopper was coming down directly in front of the *hacienda!*

"Watch it, watch it!" he snarled into the radio. "The guy is tricky! Get those fire teams in there!"

The little bird settled onto the floodlit grounds— a shiny red-and-white job with the decal of a Dallas flying service swirled across the fuselage.

Tolucci moved up behind his firing line, fidgeting with bated breath and unrelenting anticipation as the rotors spun into idle mode and the door of the helicopter swung open.

A tall figure stepped out, stooping for all possible clearance beneath those twirling blades, and stepped into the spotlights of Klingman's Wells.

He was wearing starched khakis, had a thick thatch of white hair, and was thrusting forward a very angry pioneer chin.

Blazing eyes found their focus above the heads of a crouching line of riflemen, settling upon the dismayed gaze of Jim the Animal as the old man thundered, "What the hell have you done with my girl, you nitwit!"

Bolan completed his study of the Klingman diagrams, then he draped a master chart across Jack

159

Grimaldi's leg and told him, "Spellman has the place wired for no surprises. The system wasn't operative this morning but I'm betting it is now. I'm going to need some cool navigation from you, partner."

"Lay it out," the pilot said.

"I want you to give me a running drop back here in this new construction zone." His finger was circling an area which lay between the tank farm and the Klingman security compound. "The detail map shows a trench running through here on a north–south line. They're laying a new pipeline, from the compound outward, three-foot diameter pipe. The trench is about six feet deep. I should be able to move along it with no trouble, and it will provide good cover. Some of the pipe is in place. Most of it is laid out along the trench, awaiting emplacement. I want to scout it. Maybe I can pipe myself into that compound."

Grimaldi whistled softly through the intercom. "Sounds mighty chancy," he commented.

"What isn't? The main risk will be at the inner end. There's a new pumphouse in there. I saw it this morning. Windows not in yet, lot of machinery sitting around still in the crates. I'm betting the pump is not installed yet. That could mean a pipe open at both ends, inside and outside."

"Great," the pilot said, his voice edged with sarcasm. "That gets you in . . . maybe. What gets you back out?"

Bolan was not planning a return to the drop point. The logistics would require quite a bit more than

160

mere "cool navigation." It would take an almost uncanny degree of dead-reckoning, seat-of-the-pants accuracy on the part of a damned cool pilot.

"I'll just have to seize the moment," Bolan explained. "I'll set up the diversionary fireworks and raise all the hell I can inside the compound. I'll just have to play it by ear in there."

"I could drop in and lift you out, probably."

"No, we won't push our luck on that front." Bolan tapped a large circle on the map and said, "You make the pick-up here, somewhere along this periphery. Look for my signal. Give me thirty minutes—three zero—with a ten-minute fudge limit. If I don't make the fudge, then cross your heart and beat it, and please don't send flowers."

Grimaldi scratched his cheek while scrutinizing the chart on his leg. "Okay," he said. "You're the doctor. Where do you want the equipment drop?"

Bolan's finger moved westward from the compound. "Along this line," he instructed. "Longitude doesn't matter a hell of a lot, except I'd like it as close to the depot as you can make it without being detected. Latitudinally, it has to be right along this other pipeline."

"Hey! They meet! Inside the compound!"

"Right. But the one to the depot is operational. They're pumping boo-koo barrels of crude into secret storage out there."

"Don't try that one, Sarge."

Bolan chuckled. "No worry there. The stuff moves at only about five miles per hour and I don't think I could hold my breath that long."

The pilot returned the chuckle, though some-what forced. He said, "You know . . . ? No, it's too wild."

"What?"

"If you could get into that control house . . . For the operational line, I mean. There are operator ports in there, I've seen them."

"What is that?"

"Ah, hell, this pipe-lining is a real science. They can stack those lines and call their shots, you know. So many barrels of crude, followed by so many barrels of whatever—gasoline, diesel fuel, whatever. They have dispatchers and the whole bag. On these big transcontinental lines they have switching sta-tions just like in a railroad yard. A dispatcher sits there and pushes the buttons, directing the flow here and there according to load instructions. Well, these ports, see. It's how they separate the shipments. The stuff is moving through constantly, see, stacked in there like I said with the whatevers. They mark the separation between the whatevers with a little pack-age of radioactive substance. And they have these detectors that react to the radioactivity and tells the dispatcher that here is the beginning or end of a shipment of some particular whatever. So he can route the stuff around, see, without breaking the flow."

Thoughtfully, Bolan commented, "So . . . ?"

"So those lines will move anything you want to drop in there. If you could get to one of those ports."

Bolan said, "Well, hell. That's not so wild."

"It's less than a mile from the control house to that depot, Sarge."

Bolan was skulling it. "Sure. I could drop in a timer. But hell I don't want to blow the whole damned..."

"Maybe just a small charge," Grimaldi suggested. "In a leakproof wrap. Just enough to blow one tank. Or if you're worried about touching off a runaway, maybe you could even set it to blow in the switching station out there, or somewhere along the line. It would give you some beautiful cover for your approach."

Bolan said, "Yeah. Okay. It's a great thought, Jack, thanks. I'll skull it awhile."

"This's no time for scruples," Grimaldi groused. "What the hell, a few thousand barrels of crude, what the hell."

Bolan replied, "Okay, I said I'd think about it."

Grimaldi stiffened and moved his eyes close to the windshield. "Uh oh," he muttered.

"What is it?"

"We're in the approach. And another bird is crossing our course dead ahead. It's a . . . yeah, it's another chopper."

Bolan snapped, "Change course and lay back! Let's read his intentions!"

Grimaldi killed his own navigation lights and swung into an abrupt climbing circle.

"He's circling in," the pilot reported a moment later. "He's . . . yeah. There go the landing lights. He's going down."

Bolan muttered, "It looks like he's directly over . . ."

"Yeah. He's landing inside the compound. Whups! Look at all that light, man."

The entire security compound had suddenly erupted into brilliant day-bright floodlighting.

Bolan commented, "Yep, the security is activated."

"Shit I wouldn't have your job with heaven guaranteed," the pilot said in hushed tones.

"I wouldn't either," Bolan murmured. "But that's not the guarantee, Jack. Okay, this is a good break. You'll never find a better time for that running drop. Let's start."

He was checking his weapons and stuffing last-minute armaments into the chest pouch.

"Coming around," Grimaldi reported. "Mark it thirty seconds."

"Marked. Don't stretch yourself, Jack. Forty minutes and git."

"Don't worry about that. Uh, Mack . . . in case we don't—if we don't leave this place together, you'll know where to find me any time."

Bolan gripped the pilot's shoulder and said, "Jack, you must know—I couldn't have—"

"Don't say it!" Grimaldi snapped, "Remember you said no flowers. That works both ways. Ten seconds, goddamn it."

Bolan grinned and got set.

Ten more seconds, with a hell guarantee.

Sure. It was the only way to fly.

Blue eyes flashed, the hatch slid back, and he said quietly, "Tallyho, Jack."

And he did not hear the sighing rejoinder: "Tally-ho, yourself, you beautiful bastard."

Grimaldi was aware of the guarantee on Mack Bolan's soul.

21: THE INTROSPECT

He hit the ground running, burdened with eighty pounds or more of steel and explosives, and tumbled into the ditch which had been prepared for a new pipeline.

It was a stygian night, with high stratus blotting out the heavens except for a peephole now and then with an occasional feeble starglow. It was Bolan's kind of night. He could hear Grimaldi's churning withdrawal, becoming fainter and fainter until smothered in that blackness out there; Bolan had never felt more alone in the world.

He hesitated only long enough to shake the landing shock out of his head, check his gear, adjust the load. Then he set off for the quarter-mile hike to the hell grounds.

It was slow going. The soft soil of the fresh ditch sucked at his overloaded footsteps and flowed at him from both sides with every movement.

He stopped every fifty paces or so to freeze in attentive listening, suspecting the presence of enemy patrols and relying entirely upon audio control of the situation.

Yes, it was Bolan's kind of night . . . and it was also his kind of a fight. He was one with the living unity of earth, an extension of elemental forces, and many times he had walked the blackened footpaths of darkness in an endless search for eternal day.

During an earlier stage of this survival through warfare, as a young soldier in distant lands, he had wondered at the beginning of each such trek into blackness if that "eternal day" might lay at the end of this particular mission—hoping that it did—suspecting that perhaps it never would—discovering eventually that each night march led only to another night march—learning, finally, with a reconciliation of spirit, that the night forces had taken kindly to this intrepid traveler through the gloom and had accepted him as one of their own.

The symbolic concept of "eternal day"—and the search therefor—became lost as a personal goal of this warrior. It had meant, simply, the end of warfare—the attainment of peace, human fulfillment, construction of a life instead of destruction of other lives.

The concept was buried not in Vietnam but in his own home town. Bolan's nights became transplanted from the jungles of an unpopular and improbable war to the dry deserts of a criminal and impossible war—and the Executioner had said goodbye forever to "eternal day."

A night person, sure—and Bolan had long ago pushed all the sentimental ideas about normal life and happiness off the surface of his mind. He never thought about such things, now. He no longer sought a place to live, in the sun. He now walked blackened paths and sought a place to kill, and perhaps to survive, in the night.

It was a subtle shift of psyche, this transition from

"sometime soldier" to "lifetime warrior." But it was necessary, if a guy meant to be good at his job.

Deep down where his soul reposed, Bolan was aware of all this. He was, after all, a decent man—and that innate decency had not lost touch with the larger realities, except where they touched upon his own personal ambitions for self.

And now he had reached that point where the night becomes encapsulated within a three-foot tube buried in the earth.

He took a last look into the heavens, hoping for a star and finding only a blackened reflection of his own life, and then the Executioner moved resolutely into hell itself.

22: FLASH POINT

Once again the night was with him.

The pipe ended in a large bell section at the half-completed pump station and there was nothing blocking the exit more forbidding than a plastic cover and a thin sheet of plywood.

Bolan worked his way clear and checked his numbers. Eight minutes had elapsed. Which meant that he had an outside edge of thirty-two minutes in which to outwit the security system, rout or overcome the garrison force, disable the destruct system, and tidy up a few loose ends of the night, bust out, make his way across a thousand yards of hostile territory to the depot and neutralize that area, then make the rendezvous with Grimaldi.

Nothing but precise timing could make it work; nothing short of *blitzkrieg* could make it possible.

But, sure, it was Bolan's kind of fight.

He set the deadline on his wrist chronometer and moved out without further pause, the security system diagrams overlaying his combat-consciousness like a mariner's chart of rocks and shoals.

The first obstacle loomed out of the deep dark a few yards outside the building—a slow-moving sentry with a shoulder-slung rifle. Bolan tapped him behind the ear with the butt of the Beretta and left him lay where he dropped.

169

The numbers were falling. And there was a hell of a lot to be done between now and then.

The Klingman property occupied a large section of rangeland in the Great Plains region of western Texas, just north of the Pecos River. Range livestock of several varieties grazed on these lands, sharing the productivity of the area with gypsum, salt, natural gas, and petroleum deposits. To the north and east spread the great agricultural regions which produced a variety of grains, cotton, peanuts, sorghums, poultry, hogs, melons, fruits. Far east and deep south accounted for vegetables, citrus fruits, seafoods, forest products, granite, offshore oil.

Wrapped together, this fabulous state was indeed worthy of being regarded as "the richest political subdivision in the world." As a matter of official fact, it was. It could be, if desired, a totally isolated yet entirely self-sufficient political entity—much more so than almost any European nation.

It was not difficult, then, to understand how some prideful Texans could come to regard their state's role in national and world affairs as somewhat demeaning to their importance—or the exploitation of their natural resources by "outside interests" as shameful thievery.

Klingman, himself, was one of these. Rambling notes found in the briefcase that Bolan turned over to Harold Brognola acidly denounced "the Wall Streeters and Carpetbaggers" who, in Klingman's view, were "taking Texas away from Texans and robbing us blind."

The old man had discovered, though, the hard way, that there were worse forces than Wall Streeters and Carpetbaggers afoot in the land. There were, indeed, cannibals—and they had just about eaten Arthur Klingman, whole body.

There was, of course, much more at stake in the Texas Campaign than the fate of the life and fortune of one Arthur Klingman—a man who, in any event, had damned himself. The old man had come to symbolize for Bolan, though, the entire Texas problem. Mack Bolan was not a foolish warrior. He knew his limitations, and he understood that he could not hope single-handedly to reverse, in a single night, all the unsettling developments which had come to light in this huge and complex state.

He could, though, zero-in on the fountainhead itself, and hope that the shock waves traveling along that chain of cause and effect would shake the whole structure apart. It was not a forlorn hope, but a very practical one. It was, in combat psychology, a "mission goal"—a vital target which, if properly approached and flawlessly attained, could indeed be regarded as a turning point in the larger war.

To "save Texas for the sane Texans" meant, to Mack Bolan, simply to destroy irreversibly the stranglehold which the international Mafia had succeeded in establishing at this place, in this time.

He had to run their asses out of Klingman's Wells, and he had to do it so decisively that they would not even think of returning for a long, long time.

As for the rest of Texas—well, that would be up

to Hal Brognola and the law enforcement agencies of this great state. Bolan hoped only to make the crack in the dam, the fingerhold that would allow the others to rip the whole damned thing apart.

That was the mission at Klingman's Wells, the goal of the Texas Campaign.

But there was also, as a corollary goal, a promise to be kept to a gutsy young lady with a broad Texas sense of humor.

"I'll clear a place for you in that no man's land," he'd promised her. "And I'll try to see that your daddy is standing there with you."

So the whole Bolan ideology was compressed here, in this night, at this place.

He had thought of it as a "flash point."

And it was.

Five minutes into his remaining numbers, he had disabled the electronic alarm systems. Another five minutes and the Mexican barracks plus assorted buildings were gooped for doomsday with three-minute fuses. By halfway into that fuse time, he had stealthily clubbed and garroted his way through the rear entrance of the *hacienda* and was standing in the corner of a darkened passageway which led to the large, sunken living room. Through the open double doors he had a view of a huge stone fireplace, a sparse sprinkling of Spanish-style furnishings, and four human beings.

One of these was Woofer Tolucci. A couple of small Bandaids decorated the fierce face and he seemed to be partially supporting his weight on a makeshift walking stick.

In the background stood a Mexican—a six-gun strapped to his hip, cowboy style—a very modern machine-pistol dangling on a neck strap.

Arthur was there, and only half dressed. He looked about ready to blow a gasket and he was angrily telling Tolucci something in rumbling, muffled tones.

The other half of the Klingman khaki outfit—the shirt—was adorning his daughter, Judith. It was all she wore, but it was a fetching arrangement. She stood beside her father, straight and poised as a good daughter of the Lone Star should—shirttails and all.

Whatever Klingman was saying, Tolucci evidently was not buying it. He cut off the old man's angry speech with a string of obscenities.

And then the barracks began to blow, loud rumbling explosions spaced a few seconds apart, one coming upon the other in a series that trembled the earth beneath the *hacienda* and sent Tolucci staggering toward the window.

"What the Christ!" was the head cock's initial reaction, delivered with a voice which really did not wish to know, no, not at all.

The Animal recovered quickly, though, and before the doomsday goop had fully spent its chain he was whirling toward the door and hobbling quickly off to the scene of disturbance.

"Stay here!" he yelled over his shoulder to the Mexican gunner. "If they give you any shit, shoot 'em!"

"*Si, Capitain.*"

Bolan held his position and checked Tolucci by, hardly an arm's reach away. He watched him to the outside, then Bolan stepped into the doorway of the sunken room, the Beretta extended.

The Mexican was appreciatively studying the backside of Judith Klingman as she leaned into a window sill, trying to get a view of the activities outside.

Arthur Klingman was staring straight up the bore of Mack Bolan's Beretta.

The Belle chugged a pencil of flame, something grisly happened to the Mexican's temple just above the cheekbone as a severed eye popped free and bounced to the flagstones several yards from the crumpling body.

The old man froze, stunned, as his daughter pirouetted away from the window with a little shriek. Pieces of *soldado* skull had splattered her and she was eyeing the ghastly stains with no show whatever of good humor.

Klingman mumbled, "I thought that was for me."

The icy tones of the Executioner informed him, "I'm here to save your wells, Klingman. My time is short. You'll have to get yourselves out. Give me a count of sixty after you see my back. Then you take Judith straight to the new pump station, I mean *straight!* Down through the pipe and all the way to the end. Wait for me there. I'll try to pick you up. If I'm not there in thirty minutes then you're on your own."

A fire had returned to the Klingman gaze. He told

Bolan, "I want to help. I have a right. You told me I could bury Flag Seven. Okay. Let me bury it."

"No way," Bolan replied coldly. "That's a war zone out there, Klingman. Take your girl and git! That's the best help you can give me. At the count of sixty!"

He spun away without a glance at the girl, crossed quickly to the door, and stepped outside.

People were running about out there in the glow of the burning buildings, shouting in confusion and firing weapons at the moon or something. Above it all could be heard the barking growls of the head cock yelling for someone to check out the goddamn lights and get them working.

Bolan brought added spice to that party as he moved swiftly across the edge of confusion, hurling grenades and cutting away with the chattergun at everything swirling across his line of vision.

He heard Tolucci snarl, "There he is! Miguel! Where the hell are your fire teams!"

Bolan had accomplished the immediate objective —to divert attention away from the route to be traveled by the Klingmans—and already his excursion across those hell grounds had taken a fearful toll of the enemy. Guys were lying all around those grounds, chopped up and bleeding and calling for help in Spanish. But no assistance seemed to be materializing for the luckless ones. Tolucci was regrouping his forces and shouting them on from some point in the background of action. They were trying to flank him, sending fire teams out to each side.

Bolan sprang the AutoMag and returned through the middle, throwing *blitzkrieg* to right and left in a blazing attempt to break up the countermove. The Big Thunder was packing scatter loads with 240 grains of firepower behind each round. At ten yards they would behead a man. At the present working range of twenty-five yards or so, each load would sieve a six-footer from head to toe. But it was the psychology of the big autoloading magnum that provided the greatest value in a pitched fight. It made a noise like a cannon and whatever it hit damn well stayed hit. Big Thunder would keep a lot of heads down and turn back the most determined charges.

But the numbers were running fast and there was no time to play this sort of game. Bolan assumed that the Klingmans had made their break, and he knew that it was past time for him to make his.

The Executioner quietly withdrew from the contest, falling back into the darkness and rejoining the night.

He had to get to the central control room and deactivate a doomsday device. Then he had to break westward and hit the staging depot. And he had about twenty minutes remaining in which to do it all, unless he wished to be stranded out there in enemy country. There was no guessing at what manner of opposition he was likely to encounter along the way. Somewhere out there, surely, stood a hardline force of Mafia soldiers—somewhere out there beyond the flash point, waiting for Mack Bolan's head.

But . . . this was Mack Bolan's kind of fight— fast on the numbers, hit and git and never look back.

It was the only way for a one man army to operate, if it meant to keep on operating.

The Executioner meant to keep on keeping on. His war, he hoped, was a long way from over.

Texas was a long way from over.

23: BURIED

Bolan discovered very quickly the whereabouts of the "hardliners." They had been deployed in and around the control building and, yeah, it was a head party.

Not a one, apparently, had ventured away from his assigned station to investigate the hullabaloo in the billeting area. They were poised and waiting for a pigeon to blunder it—and they numbered at least a baker's dozen.

The only way was a thunder punch, straight up the middle. He shed all extraneous gear, tossed a smoke bomb to dead center, heaved a percussion grenade to either side, and ran the gauntlet in a balls-out sprint, the AutoMag in rapid fire straight ahead.

An immediate volley with handguns greeted the daring challenge, fire triangulating on his path from both sides and a rather weak return from dead ahead—then he was into the smoke and the grenades were pummeling the night on his flanks.

He hit the door at full gallop, moving in with a puff of smoke and a fresh clip in Big Thunder. Two boys with shrinking eyes fell away from there, stumbling backwards into the building and jerking off their shots much too carelessly. The .44 magnum boomed in reflexive response, roaring twice and hurl-

178

ing those boys aside like so much ground meat on the hoof.

Another guy stood up quickly from behind a control console and made an exaggerated show of lowering a pistol to the floor. He was wearing technician's white coveralls and his voice held a Texas sound as he hastily reported to the invader, "*Wait*, mister, I just work here!"

A gunshot sounded from Bolan's rear and a slug whistled past him and caromed off a piece of equipment. He swiveled and sent three quick rounds into the doorway. A guy fell back out of there screaming in an explosion of glass and shredded metal.

Bolan moved out of the line-up and coolly told the technician, "You're working for me, now. I want the heart out of that doomsday device. Don't try to screw me around and maybe you can live to tell your grandchildren about this. I've seen the schematics. I know what I want."

The guy didn't even think about it. He went straight to a panel in the back wall, pulled out a sliding chassis, and began disconnecting wires.

The time required for the operation was less than a minute, during which Bolan discouraged another rush on the door with three big booms of the Auto-Mag.

It was the last of the scatter loads. He ejected the empty clip and snapped in a reload of heart-stoppers as the guy in white delivered the control chassis from the demolitions network.

Bolan said, "Yeah, that's it." He dropped it to the floor and sent a pair of big .44 slugs smashing into it, then he told the guy, "Okay, show me the soft way out."

"There's a fire door in back."

Bolan sent the technician an almost smile. "Thanks," he said. "Here's a souvenir." He flipped a medal and the guy caught it. Then Bolan made fast tracks to the rear.

It was the type of door with a quick-release lever running the entire width. He hit the lever with a foot and went right on through in a twisting leap, hitting the ground outside at full prone and sending somebody out there sprawling with him.

A pistol flared, almost in his face. He felt the heat from the muzzle and sensed the passage of whistling metal past his nose at the same instant that he squeezed into his own pull, the thunder of the Auto-Mag eclipsing the report of the other gun.

The guy beside him caught his breath and held it, the pistol skittered away, and Bolan knew immediately that he was lying down with Woofer Tolucci.

Another shadowy form was cautiously approaching. Bolan angled the thunderpiece two degrees right and let go again. The guy went over backwards without a sound and stayed there.

Bolan stayed there, too, waiting for his eyes to readjust to darkness and trying to orient himself to the environment. There was a ringing in his ears and he knew that he'd taken a bit too much audio from Tolucci's weapon.

He was partially disabled, momentarily anyway. The Animal was breathing again, but with difficulty. Bolan told him, "End of the line, Woofer."

"Don't kill me," Tolucci groaned. "I can make it."

"You're dead already, guy."

"No! Just my leg. I think you blew it off."

Almost, but not quite. Bolan's reflex round had smashed in just above the guy's knee, and it had made a hell of a mess. The pain must have been next to unendurable, but the big animal was not complaining about that. He wanted only to survive.

"Call it even, smartass. It's twice you got me. So okay, I'm ready for pasture. I swear, I'm finished in the business, anyway."

Bolan knew better. Guys like Tolucci were never finished, until they were buried.

People were moving around out there, cautiously, setting up. Bolan shook his head, willing it to find its motor.

"I swear," Tolucci groaned.

Then another sound stole between the two grounded men. It was a reedy, electronically distorted voice issuing from a small, two-way radio which lay between them. Bolan had heard that voice before, very recently. It was Lileo.

"Woofer! What's going on down there? What's all the fires?"

Tolucci snarled, "Oh Christ!"

"Woofer, damn it answer! We're coming in. What's the situation there?"

The Animal tried to raise himself to an elbow but fell quickly back with a moan. "That runway is mined," he woofed. "Tell 'em, Bolan. Don't let them land."

181

Bolan picked up the radio, put on his street voice, and reported to the headshed. "That guy is runnin' wild down here, sir. We need help, quick!"

"Who is this? Where's Woofer?"

"He's down, sir. We're catchin' hell!"

"Light that runway!"

"Can't, sir. The guy killed all the outside lighting. But you better hurry." Bolan held the transmission button open and squeezed off another round from the AutoMag, then thumbed-off and tossed the radio away.

"You lousy bastard," Tolucci groaned.

"Yeah," Bolan agreed, and shot the suffering animal squarely between the eyes.

Then he raised his voice in a fair imitation of Tolucci's and screamed, "Get down to the airstrip! Wave 'em off, damn it! They don't know it's mined! It's Lileo's force, don't let them land!"

Someone screamed back, "Use th' radio, boss!"

"You asshole, it's shot up! *Get down there!*"

There were immediate sounds of movement and someone called, "Mr. Tolucci?"

"Yeh, yeh, I'm awright! It's just my goddam fuckin' leg! I got Bolan! Now get down there and wave off that plane!"

Bolan knew that all the king's men could not stop that landing.

But people were scrambling, and this time with relief and abandon and in the pursuit of a desperate mission.

Bolan came to his knees as the last fuzzy forms

faded away, and tried to focus his eyes on the dial of the wrist chronometer.

His numbers had fallen to hell. Less than ten minutes remained. So how now, big bad Bolan? Did he throw it all to hell and go on with the depot hit? Or did he scrub out, and hope for another time?

He was opting toward the latter and pulling himself wearily together when another dark form materialized from the darkness, stepping into the open, arm extended, pistol in hand.

He was big, like Texas, and his name was Arthur Klingman.

In a voice nearly as icy as Bolan's, the old man was saying, "I told you I'd kill you, Tolucci."

Bolan checked his squeeze and quickly replied, "You're a bit late. The Animal is dead."

The gun arm dropped immediately and the big Texan moved in to stand tall above the kneeling man in blacksuit. "I damn near blasted you. I thought I heard—oh, that was you."

"It was me. I thought I sent you home."

"You sent Judith. I stayed behind to bury Flag Seven."

Bolan said, "Congratulations." The numbed sections of his brain were coming alive again. He got to his feet and hooked an arm into Klingman's and said, "There's just time, maybe, to get an airlift out of here. We have to breach the fence and get out near the staging area."

Klingman was allowing himself to be hurried across the grounds but he had vocal objections. "It isn't safe out there. I told you. I'm burying it."

183

"What does that mean?"

"It means I sent a shipment out. It should be arriving in a few minutes."

"Through the pipe?"

"That's right. It's set to go off in the main distribution tank. There's more than oil out there, Bolan. I told you. It's an ammunition dump, too. When that high tank goes, it's going to take a hell of a lot of everything out there with it. I also programmed a load for relay into the gasoline storage, vehicle area."

The two refugees from hell had come to a halt on high ground near the west fence. Bolan said, "A *load?*"

"Yeah. Explosives, incendiary. That whole place will be an inferno within another five minutes or so."

Bolan mentally tipped his hat to Jack Grimaldi. So okay, it could be done and Arthur Klingman was trying it.

The Executioner was thinking about that and gazing back upon the low ground when a bright flash lit up the landing strip, for one brief instant outlining in brilliant relief a two-engine transport plane which had apparently just touched down. The moment moved on, the aircraft became an exploding part of that brilliance and sent a fireball whoofing skyward, and Bolan muttered, "Goodbye, Bolan Bunch."

More than Flag Seven was getting a burial at Klingman's Wells.

Bolan rolled a percussion grenade toward a post

of the electrified fence and pushed the old man to the ground in anticipation of that blast.

They moved quickly through the gap and joined the darkness at the backside of the rise, and Bolan got his star shell ready for the signal to Grimaldi.

Then he heard him. The guy was up there, hovering somewhere high in the blackness in direct disobedience of orders. Bolan could hear the eggbeater punishing the air up there, directly overhead.

The hot-wing guy had probably had them in sight all the way across those grounds, spotting them with the fires of the compound.

And he'd just earned himself a long vacation wherever he wanted it, with all the Mafia bucks at Bolan's disposal.

Bolan squeezed the old man's arm, said, "Not every thing is getting buried at the wells tonight, Klingman," and let fly the signal flare.

Texas, by God, was not getting buried there.

EPILOGUE

They tracked over to the north–south pipeline and took Judith Klingman on board, then rose high for a bird's eye view of the big storm on the Texas plains.

The fires were burning out in the Klingman compound. Even the twisted mess on the airstrip had been reduced to a feeble glow.

Over to the west, though, the show was just beginning. The night lit up over there several seconds before the shock waves set the little bird to rocking, and thunder rumbled across the land.

Great streaming streakers of flaming liquid catapulted skyward like a Fourth of July fireworks fountain, and raging lakes of fire spilled everywhere in a consuming flood.

Another fantastic explosion in the vehicle area sent a column of flame higher than Grimaldi's bird, and hell took a march across those haunted acres.

They moved closer, with caution, and Bolan watched through binoculars as men swarmed like ants in panic in the midst of the inferno.

"There's your picnic, boys," he muttered.

The most satisfying part, to Bolan's mind, was that a tough old Texan had laid the picnic spread.

Klingman's eyes were watering, though, as he turned away from the spectacle. "Rest in peace," he intoned in a rumbling voice.

Bolan donned the headset and told Grimaldi, "That's all the tally I've got, Jack. Let's pull out."

Grimaldi smiled sourly and heeled eastward. He told the Executioner, "You might enjoy something I heard on the radio a few minutes ago, just the same. Massive police raids all over the state. The news guy says a special federal force is calling the shots. Sounds like a clean sweep."

"Yeah," Bolan said. "Let's hope so." But his tone did not sound so hopeful. He was all too familiar with the great American circus of political influence and clouted courts. "A start, anyway," he concluded.

Judith Klingman leaned forward suddenly and rubbed his back with a soft touch, then spoke her first words of the evening to Mack Bolan. "You're bleeding," she gasped.

"Imagine that," he growled.

"You need a doctor!"

"I know a good one," Bolan said, sliding a tired grin toward Grimaldi. "What I really need is a good nurse. For about three days of R&R." If he was bleeding, then it could be no more than a battle scratch. More than likely it was enemy blood. He swiveled about to regard the girl with an Executioner stare. "Can you recommend some one for the job?"

Her gaze fell from that probing inspection and she replied, "I'm not much of a nurse, I guess." The eyes flared up, defiantly. "But I'm pretty damn good at R&R. Are you?"

He grinned and said, "I'll bet."

So this one was winding up, maybe, in a little shaft of sunlight—starshine, anyway. The Executioner had won another brief victory. He was among friends, for a while. The Heart of Texas was bursting forth within that beautiful young lady behind him. And, sure, he had to do *something* between here and Detroit.

"Take the young lady to her rest and recreation area, Jack," he told the pilot.

A small hand crept along his side and nestled his arm. "And her knight," Judith Klingman commanded.

"What night?" Bolan asked, too weary to think.

"Knight." She spelled it. "The one with the shining eyes—and no armor, no armor at all."

Bolan took that hand and held it, and let all the tension go as his over-used frame settled into the seat cushion in total repose.

If this was damnation, then he'd earned it.

Yeah.

the EXECUTIONER
by Don Pendleton

DEATH MERCHANT

by Joseph Rosenberger

Richard Camellion is a master of disguise, deception, and destruction. He gets the dirty jobs, the operations that cannot be handled by the FBI, the CIA, or any other legal or extralegal force. He loves his job...and his job is death.

Over 2.5 million copies sold!

☐	40-483-2	Death Merchant	#1	$1.50
☐	40-417-4	Operation Overkill	#2	1.50
☐	40-458-1	Psychotron Plot	#3	1.50
☐	40-418-2	Chinese Conspiracy	#4	1.50
☐	40-419-0	Satan Strike	#5	1.50
☐	40-459-X	Albanian Connection	#6	1.50
☐	40-420-4	The Castro File	#7	1.50
☐	40-421-2	Billionaire Mission	#8	1.50
☐	220594-6	Laser War	#9	1.25
☐	220473-3	Mainline Plot	#10	1.25
☐	220561-5	Manhattan Wipeout	#11	1.25
☐	220642-3	KGB Frame	#12	1.25
☐	40-497-2	Mato Grosso Horror	#13	1.50
☐	220796-7	Vengeance: Golden Hawk	#14	1.25
☐	220823-9	Iron Swastika Plot	#15	1.25
☐	220857-7	Invasion of Clones	#16	1.25
☐	220880-9	Zemlya Expedition	#17	1.25
☐	220911-2	Nightmare in Algeria	#18	1.25
☐	40-460-3	Armageddon, USA!	#19	1.50
☐	40-256-2	Hell in Hindu Land	#20	1.50
☐	40-019-6	Pole Star Secret	#21	1.25
☐	40-043-6	Kondrashev Chase	#22	1.25
☐	40-078-5	Budapest Action	#23	1.25
☐	40-352-6	Kronos Plot	#24	1.50
☐	40-117-8	Enigma Project	#25	1.25
☐	40-118-3	Mexican Hit	#26	1.50
☐	40-119-1	Surinam Affair	#27	1.50
☐	40-254-6	Nipponese Nightmare	#28	1.50

PINNACLE—BOOK MAILING SERVICE
Box 690, Rockville Centre, N.Y. 11571

Please send me the books I have checked above. I am enclosing $ _____ (please add 50¢ to cover postage and handling). Send check or money order—no cash or C.O.D.'s please.

Name _____

Address_____

City _____ State/Zip _____

Please allow approximately four weeks for delivery.

THE Penetrator

by Lionel Derrick

Mark Hardin is a warrior without uniform or rank, pledged to fight anyone on either side of the law who seeks to destroy the American way of life.

Over 1.5 million copies sold!

☐	40-101-2	Target is H	# 1	$1.25
☐	40-102-0	Blood on the Strip	# 2	1.25
☐	40-422-0	Capitol Hell	# 3	1.50
☐	40-423-9	Hijacking Manhattan	# 4	1.50
☐	40-424-7	Mardi Gras Massacre	# 5	1.50
☐	40-493-X	Tokyo Purple	# 6	1.50
☐	40-494-8	Baja Bandidos	# 7	1.50
☐	40-495-6	Northwest Contract	# 8	1.50
☐	40-425-5	Dodge City Bombers	# 9	1.50
☐	220690-2	Hellbomb Flight	# 10	1.25
☐	220728-0	Terror in Taos	# 11	1.25
☐	220797-5	Bloody Boston	# 12	1.25
☐	40-426-3	Dixie Death Squad	# 13	1.50
☐	40-427-1	Mankill Sport	# 14	1.50
☐	220882-5	Quebec Connection	# 15	1.25
☐	220912-0	Deepsea Shootout	# 16	1.25
☐	40-456-5	Demented Empire	# 17	1.50
☐	40-428-X	Countdown to Terror	# 18	1.50
☐	40-429-8	Panama Power Play	# 19	1.50
☐	40-258-9	Radiation Hit	# 20	1.50
☐	40-079-3	Supergun Mission	# 21	1.25
☐	40-067-5	High Disaster	# 22	1.50
☐	40-085-3	Divine Death	# 23	1.50
☐	40-177-9	Cryogenic Nightmare	# 24	1.50
☐	40-178-7	Floating Death	# 25	1.50
☐	40-179-5	Mexican Brown	# 26	1.50